"You deserve someone much better than me."

He stepped forward. "But, Kate—"

"No." She stepped back, raising her hands in the air. "You're not weakening my resolve to take care of my own problems. This time I have to make things right myself."

"I get it, but it doesn't mean I like it."

"I'm really sorry, Jack. I don't know what else to say."

"Well, can I at least give you a hug before you leave?"

Her lip trembled and she nodded, moving into his open arms.

He held her close, her head resting against his chest. He stroked her hair, savoring the silky texture and inhaling her distinctive scent. It felt so right to hold her close in his arms, and he forced himself to pull away.

NARELLE ATKINS

lives in Canberra, Australia, with her husband and children. Her love of romance novels was inspired by her grandmother's extensive collection. After discovering inspirational romances, she decided to write stories of faith and romance. A regular at her local gym, she also enjoys traveling and spending time with family and friends.

NARELLE ATKINS

Falling for the Farmer

HEARTSONG
PRESENTS

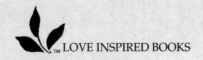

LOVE INSPIRED BOOKS

Recycling programs for this product may not exist in your area.

ISBN-13: 978-0-373-48698-4

FALLING FOR THE FARMER

Copyright © 2014 by Narelle Atkins

www.Harlequin.com

Printed in U.S.A.

For it is by grace you have been saved, through faith—and this is not from yourselves, it is the gift of God—not by works, so that no one can boast.
—*Ephesians* 2:8–9

For my husband, Jay, and my children who are an immense joy and blessing in my life. I love you.

I appreciate the encouragement and support I've received from many people during the writing of this book. Mary Hawkins, my amazing mentor and dear friend. Susan Diane Johnson and Stacy Monson, my fabulous critique partners who have helped me grow as a writer. Many thanks to Laura O'Connell for her challenging critiques, the generous ladies on the Faith, Hope and Love "Finish the Book" loop for their wisdom and encouragement, and my Aussie writing friends from Omega Writers who are passionate supporters of Australian Christian authors.

I thank my reader friends for their helpful feedback and support: Jen B, Lisa B, Raylee B, Karinne C, Tracey H, Heather M, Merlyn S and Nicky S. Thanks also to Jim S for providing invaluable research opportunities. The original idea for this book was born during a visit to his apple orchards.

A special thank you to my editor, Kathy Davis, and the team at Harlequin.

Chapter 1

She had to escape now!

The long aisle surrounded by rows of smiling faces awaited Kate Lawson as she paused for photos at the back of the church, her sweaty hand clutching her father's tuxedo-clad forearm.

Her fiancé stood at the end of the aisle, a triumphant grin on his face as his gaze swept over the crowded church.

Her father's eyes misted. "You're doing great."

Kate shook her head. "Dad, I'm sorry. I can't do this." She lifted her wedding dress off the plush carpet and ran out of the church, her low heels scraping the stone steps as she sprinted to the bridal car.

Gulping air into her burning lungs, she wrenched open the cumbersome passenger door of the Cadillac and threw her bridal bouquet on the floor. She slid onto the soft cream leather seat, the full skirt of her gown settling over her legs.

Jack Bradley spun around in the driver's seat, his tawny-brown eyes widening after she pulled the door closed and fastened her seat belt.

Her pulse raced and she sucked in a shallow breath. "Let's go."

"Where? Why?" He stashed his phone in the dashboard console. "Aren't you supposed to be inside the church getting married?"

Kate glanced out the rear window. Her mother hobbled down the church steps in three-inch heels, her crimson face glowing in the late-morning Sydney sunshine. "Please, Jack, I'll tell you later."

He switched on the ignition and the powerful engine rumbled to life. He drove out of the church parking lot, slowing to maneuver his prized Cadillac Eldorado through the narrow gate.

She gripped the skirt bunched on her lap, refusing to look back at the church and her mother. Jack needed to put his foot down on the accelerator and get her out of here. *Now.*

He merged into a gap in the traffic. "Where are we going?"

"Anywhere. I don't care." She hadn't thought that far ahead. From the moment she had walked into the church and spotted Rodney's smug face at the altar, fleeing the wedding had become her sole objective.

He pulled up at a traffic light and she flicked her veil back over her shoulder, meeting Jack's speculative gaze.

His mouth curved up in a slight smile. "I guess you're not having a good day."

She lowered her lashes, certain she was experiencing one of the worst days of her twenty-three years. "What do you think?"

"Your mother looked furious. Are you sure you want to do this? I could turn around—"

"No!" Her hands trembled in her lap. "It's too late now to change my mind."

What had she done? Running from the church on her wedding day wasn't something she'd ever thought she'd be capable of doing. Or want to do.

She massaged her temples, a dull ache starting to pound her head. The white ribbon attached to the front of the car stayed firm in the breeze, unlike her tumultuous thoughts.

Jack stopped at the next light. "Do you want to go to my sister's place?"

She nodded. Megan, her maid of honor, would hopefully realize her Chatswood apartment was Kate's logical destination.

"Are you okay?" His eyes softened and his questioning gaze held a look of genuine concern.

She blinked away the moisture building in her eyes. "I need to think, and work out what to do." All her plans for the next few months had disappeared the moment she left the church. Where would she live? She'd need to find a new job.

Jack swung his Cadillac onto the highway, heading toward the northern Sydney suburb of Chatswood.

She rubbed her teeth over her lower lip. "Do you know how to get to Megan's apartment from here?"

"Of course. I also have a spare key since I left some of my gear at her place."

"Are you staying overnight?"

He shook his head. "You can have the lumpy sofa bed tonight. I was going to head straight back to the farm after you were safely delivered to your wedding reception. But I guess I have an early mark."

She wrung her hands together in her lap, glad her purse

and luggage were stowed in the boot. One less problem she'd need to worry about later.

"I'm curious," he said. "Were you planning to run before you arrived at the church?"

"Not really." The thought had entered her head this morning, the fantasy of escaping a life she didn't want tormenting her as the wedding ceremony grew closer. She had stepped inside the church, and realized she couldn't make vows in God's sight to love Rodney forever. "I couldn't go through with it." She paused. "And I know what you're thinking."

His eyes widened as he waited for her response.

"I should have canceled the wedding earlier." And she should never have accepted Rodney's marriage proposal in the first place.

She stared out the passenger window. Groups of people strolled along the sidewalk, drinking takeaway coffee and ducking in and out of shops and cafés. Today was probably just another ordinary Saturday in their lives. She closed her eyes. She couldn't undo what she had done and it was too late now to worry about what might have been.

"What about your former fiancé? I'm sure he's not feeling too great right now."

She dipped her head, feeling the full impact of the embarrassment and distress she'd inflicted on her ex-fiancé. "I know. It's all a big disaster."

She twisted her veil off her head and shook her hair loose. Dark brown locks of wavy hair spilled over her shoulders, covering the beading on the bodice of her ivory gown.

Sunlight glinted on the enormous diamond engagement ring she'd moved to her right hand earlier this morning. Its brilliance taunted her, a cruel reminder of the distressing chain of events she'd set in motion.

Ripples of fear swirled in her belly. She didn't want to face her mother's fury. During the week her mother had refused to listen to or acknowledge her concerns about marrying Rodney. It seemed like her mother was more enamored with Kate's ex-fiancé than she'd ever been.

She drew in a deep breath. Rodney needed to face the truth: she'd been pushed into this marriage and short engagement. Her mother had taken over, making all the wedding arrangements with the exception of the cars. A suitable white Cadillac couldn't be found in Sydney at short notice and, much to her mother's horror, Kate had enlisted Megan's help in organizing the hire of Jack's maroon Cadillac. It was her only rebellion against her mother's wedding regime…until today.

She'd been a reluctant bride and now she was a runaway bride. How humiliating!

A few days ago Rodney had killed any spark of love she may have felt for him. Now that she was free, she was certain she had made the right decision.

They crawled along in the late-Saturday-morning traffic. Kate lowered the window, inhaling car fumes. The autumn weather had turned warm and the Cadillac convertible, in original condition, didn't boast air-conditioning.

Jack sat comfortably in the driver's seat, his crisp, white, linen shirt covering well-defined biceps. His strong jaw looked good in profile, and his sun-streaked hair was neatly clipped above the cuff of his collar. Work-hardened hands, tanned from laboring outdoors in his apple orchards, gave away the fact he toiled on the land for a living.

His shoulders were broader than she remembered from his days as a university student in Sydney. Back then he'd seemed oblivious to her teenage crush, and had been devoted to his beautiful, longtime girlfriend and childhood sweetheart.

Skyscraper office towers loomed ahead. She hoped Megan would guess her plan and realize she'd take refuge in her apartment. She didn't dare contact Megan in case her mother was nearby. Her phone, stowed in the boot with her luggage, was switched off and she assumed she had dozens of messages awaiting her attention. Messages she'd prefer not to read.

Jack's phone beeped.

Her stomach tightened. "Has Megan sent you a message?"

An upcoming traffic light turned red and he slowed, checking his phone when the car came to a halt. "Yep. I'll pull over up ahead and read it." He found a parking spot that accommodated the Cadillac.

Kate drummed her fingers on the wooden paneling, not caring that she might chip her manicured nails. "What did she say?"

"Don't panic. She can meet us at her apartment."

She stifled a giggle. Hysteria was threatening to take over. "Sounds good."

Relief filled her heart and she drew in a few steadying breaths. Megan was clearheaded and decisive. She'd also be supportive of Kate's decision to run once she learned the truth. Just before they'd entered the church, Megan had asked her if she was certain she was making the right decision.

She frowned. If only she'd ignored her mother's advice and confided her fears to her best friend.

Jack drove the Cadillac into a visitor parking space outside Megan's high-rise apartment complex.

Kate flung open the door and bundled her skirts out of the car.

"Hey, let me help you." He walked around to her side of the car.

She hiked up her dress. "I'm fine."

"But you're dragging your skirt over the pavement."

She clenched the silky fabric in her fists. "I hate this dress and I don't care if it gets ruined."

He stood in front of her, blocking her path. "You need to calm down. I don't want you breaking your neck crossing the car park."

She closed her eyes, counting to ten. Breathe in, breathe out. It wasn't his fault that she was in this predicament. He had indulged her desire to leave the church in a hurry and he deserved her thanks, not her anger.

"Jack, I'm sorry." Tears threatened to fill her eyes. "I don't know how to thank you for everything you've done today."

He shrugged. "Just don't hurt yourself whilst you're on my watch, okay?" His gaze travelled over her dress.

She nodded, a shiver of anticipation galloping up her spine.

"I hate to say it, but I agree with you."

She lifted a brow. "Really?"

His eyes twinkled. "You look like a sparkly meringue."

She laughed and cracked a genuine smile. "It's a horrible dress, isn't it?"

"I assume it wasn't your choice."

"My mother had her heart set on this dress. I wanted to wear something sleeker and more sophisticated but she insisted on this overdone and billowing satin concoction."

"That's one way of putting it."

She wrinkled her nose. "And it's totally unflattering."

He shook his head. "Despite the dress, you look gorgeous. Even that dress can't hide your beauty."

Heat rose in her cheeks, enveloping her face. "You're just saying that to make me feel better."

His smile widened and a familiar white sedan drove into the lot. Megan leaped out of the car and ran over to Kate.

"Are you okay?" Megan asked. "I couldn't believe it when I reached the end of the aisle and realized you'd run out the door."

"I know." She lowered her lashes. "Sensible Kate doesn't usually behave like this."

"And then there was chaos in the church. Speaking of which, we need to go inside before your mother and ex-fiancé work out where you are." She turned to her brother. "Hey, thanks for saving the day. We owe you."

"No problem," he said. "I didn't do much."

Megan shook her head. "You drove her away from that jerk. Can you please grab Kate's luggage while I help her upstairs?"

He nodded. "I'll be right behind you."

Kate lifted up the front section of her dress to stop herself from tripping on the hem. "I don't know how I managed to run to the car without falling over."

"Divine intervention, I think," Megan said. "Good thinking to stash your luggage at the last minute in the Cadillac." She frowned. "Why didn't you tell me you were planning to run?"

"Meg, I'm sorry." She stepped inside the apartment building and Megan called an elevator. "I felt like I was drowning in a wave of activity all morning and then in the church I had a moment of clarity and knew what I needed to do."

"Hey, don't apologize for not making a massive mistake."

"You don't like Rodney, do you?"

Megan pressed her lips together. Jack joined them and they moved forward into the elevator. Megan pushed the button for the eighth floor and the lift started to rise. She turned and looked Kate straight in the eye. "I don't think he's the right man for you and I'm glad you can see that now."

The door opened and they walked out into the hall. Megan unlocked her apartment door and they all piled inside.

Kate turned to Jack. "Thanks for bringing up my luggage."

He smiled. "You're welcome. Where do you want the bags?"

"My bedroom," Megan said. "Kate, do you need help getting changed?"

She nodded. "I'm trapped by all the buttons down the back of the dress."

She walked into Megan's bedroom and inhaled Jack's distinctive aftershave as he left the room.

After closing the bedroom door, Megan made quick work of undoing all the tiny buttons. Kate's dress fell into a big mess on the floor around her.

Her thoughts turned to Jack. She sucked in a deep breath, shaking her head. What was she doing, thinking about Jack? She was in enough trouble today without creating more. He was undeniably an attractive man, even more so than she remembered, but the absolute last thing she should be contemplating was another disastrous romantic entanglement.

The engagement ring slid easily off her finger and she stored it in her purse. Later she'd return the ring to Rodney. She slipped on a pair of jeans and a T-shirt before heading into the spacious living room of Megan's apartment.

Jack lounged on the sofa, an oversize coffee mug in his hand.

"Are you hungry?" Megan asked. "I'll make sandwiches and brew a pot of tea, unless you want something stronger?"

She shook her head and curled up in an overstuffed armchair. "I'm not hungry but tea sounds good."

Megan walked back into the open-plan kitchen.

Kate met Jack's warm gaze.

"Feel better now?" he asked.

"Yeah, except I have no idea what I'm going to do. Dad's cool but I couldn't bear to live at home with my mother after today's events."

"You could stay here," Megan said. "I'll be at the ski slopes for the whole season and my room will be empty. I'm sure my roomies won't mind."

She shook her head. "I haven't got a job and my savings won't last long."

"With your skills you should pick up something soon," Megan said.

Jack sipped his coffee. "What type of work do you do?"

"Accounts clerk, reception, office work. But here's the thing. My mother only lives three suburbs away and she's going to make my life miserable after she spent so much money and time organizing the wedding."

Megan placed a platter of sandwiches on the coffee table. "I didn't think of that."

"I need to get away, and have some time to think and work out what I want to do with my life."

Jack sat up straighter in his seat, inspecting the selection of sandwiches. "Why don't you go to the snow with Megan?"

Megan clapped her hands together. "Of course. Why didn't I think of that? I have a twin room to myself and you can hang out with me, hit the slopes and use that gorgeous ski gear you purchased for your European honeymoon."

Kate nibbled her lower lip. "I don't know."

The doorbell pealed, interrupting the conversation.

Megan rose and answered the intercom.

Kate's father's deep voice boomed through the intercom. "Is Katie with you?"

"She's here," Megan said.

"Is it okay if her mother and I come up?"

Megan lifted a brow.

Kate nodded. She couldn't put off seeing her mother forever.

Megan buzzed them in and before long a brisk knock sounded on the apartment door.

Kate stood. "I'll get the door."

She pulled the door open. Her mother's blazing eyes scorched her and she took a step back.

"How dare you," her mother said. "I raised you better than this." She stalked into the room, her gaze zeroing in on Jack.

"And you," her mother said, pointing at Jack. "This fiasco is your fault!"

Chapter 2

Kate gasped. "Mother!"

Jack stood. "You're wrong." He crossed his arms over his broad chest. "Kate chose to leave the church and I followed her directions."

"But I employed you to drive her to the church and reception, not to help her run away!" Kate's mother stamped her foot like a petulant child.

"This isn't Jack's fault," Kate said.

Kate's father grasped her mother's arm. "Ann, you need to calm down and start being reasonable."

Ann stared at Kate, her mouth pulled into a thin line. "Young lady, get your wedding dress back on. I spoke to the pastor and he said he can marry you and Rodney at the reception venue. It's not ideal but—"

"I'm not marrying Rodney." Kate stood beside her father and gripped his hand. "Dad, please understand I can't do this." She was no longer a child her mother could order around.

Her father nodded. "No one is going to make you get married today."

"But Philip," her mother screeched. "All the arrangements have been made and our guests are waiting at the church for an answer. I refuse to be publicly humiliated because of our daughter's selfishness."

Kate shut her eyes, feeling like a knife had pierced through her ribs and into her heart. Her mother knew exactly what to say to make her feel guilty.

"Mom, I'm sorry—"

"Then prove it." Ann walked to the entrance of Megan's bedroom, frowning at the crumpled wedding dress on the floor. "I'll help you get dressed and fix your hair. Where did you put your veil?"

Kate sucked in a deep breath. "You're not listening to me. You can't make me change my mind about the wedding."

"Now Kate, you're making the biggest mistake of your life." Ann lowered her voice and linked her arm through her daughter's arm. "You know I have your best interests at heart and when you calm down and think everything through you'll realize I'm right."

"No, I won't." She broke away from her mother, her breathing hard and fast.

Jack cleared his throat and pinned her mother with an unflinching gaze. "Kate has said no and I think you should leave."

"Yes, I agree," her father said. He turned to Kate. "Are you coming home tonight?"

She shook her head, her decision about the next few months now clear in her mind. "I'll stay here tonight then leave Sydney with Megan tomorrow or Monday."

"What?" her mother yelled. "You can't just pack up and leave. You need to talk with Rodney and sort out whatever misunderstanding has happened."

Kate frowned. "Has it ever crossed your mind that he might hate me right now and never want to see me again?" She didn't look forward to facing Rodney anytime soon.

Ann narrowed her eyes. "But he loves you and would do anything for you."

"Including letting me go?" She pressed her fingers to her forehead, hoping to relieve the throbbing pain in her temples. "Look, if he calls I'll talk to him, but I don't want to see him in person."

"All right. I guess that's a start," Ann said.

Her father grabbed hold of her mother's hand. "Katie, we'll leave now and we'll be out this afternoon if you need to go home and collect a few things."

"Thanks, Dad." She attempted a smile, tears pricking her eyes.

He nodded. "Please call me and let me know you're okay."

"I will."

Her father escorted her mother out of the apartment and Kate collapsed into an armchair.

Megan let out a low whistle. "Your mother is a piece of work."

"Now do you believe me?" She stood, too much nervous energy flowing through her to sit still. "I've spent too many years trying to please her by doing what she thinks is best."

"I'm excited you're coming to the snow. And since I'm borrowing your car, you'll have transport while you're there."

She nodded, switching on her phone. Rodney had given her a brand-new convertible as a wedding present. It sat in his garage and was registered in his name. Thankfully, she had decided to lend her old car to Megan instead of selling it like Rodney had suggested.

Jack glanced at his watch. "I'm going to take off soon, if you two are okay?"

"Sure," Megan said. "Kate, how many messages do you have?"

"Dozens, but if I'm right about my mother she'll be on the phone to Rodney right now and he'll call me in the next few minutes."

Jack raised an eyebrow. "Really? If I was in his shoes, that's the last thing I'd be doing."

A musical chime vibrated from Kate's phone and she checked the caller ID. "It's him." She frowned and headed to Megan's bedroom.

Kate closed the door to Megan's room, and Jack shook his head. "That's one crazy family."

"Tell me about it." Megan poured herself a cup of tea. "I'm so proud of Kate for standing up to her mother."

"I don't get it. You're happy that a whole bunch of people have been inconvenienced today, including me."

"I made sure you got paid very well for this job."

"Yeah, but I was up before four this morning." He stifled a yawn. "I could have slept in, maybe played touch football this afternoon with the boys."

"My guess, big brother, is that you would have been up at dawn and doing something in the orchards, anyway."

He grinned. "With Mom and Dad away, and the chauffeur business taking off, I hardly have any spare time. I'm ten foot under in paperwork and avoiding the office."

"Does Mom know?"

"I don't want to bother her." Their mother had enough to worry about, caring for their sick grandfather in Queensland.

Megan sipped her tea. "Kate's been gone awhile. I hope she hasn't changed her mind."

"I doubt it. She looked pretty determined." Kate had been like his little sister when he'd been in college in Sydney. And the pretty young girl he remembered was all grown up now and standing up to her nightmare mother.

He'd been shocked by her dramatic appearance in his Cadillac at the church, although she had seemed nervous during the drive to the church. Megan had sat beside him, chatting away while Kate was quiet, occasionally speaking in low tones with her father in the back.

He still couldn't fathom why she didn't cancel the wedding earlier, despite witnessing her mother's over-the-top performance. Kate's stunning, clear blue eyes had clouded with tears a few times but she'd held them in check and somehow managed to hold herself together.

Kate had grown into a beautiful woman, but from today's events it was obvious she wasn't particularly reliable when it came to her personal life. He knew what it felt like to lose someone he loved when he thought their relationship was strong and had a future. He'd never met her ex-fiancé but he couldn't help feeling a little bit sorry for him. How could a man trust a woman who ran out on him at the last possible moment, leaving him humiliated in front of family and friends?

Rodney would be a fool to want Kate back after what she'd done. There's no way in the world he'd give a woman like Kate a second chance if she pulled a stunt like that on him.

Kate reappeared in the living room, small worry lines forming between her brows.

Megan leaped to her feet. "Is everything okay?"

She nodded. "He wants me back but I said no."

His jaw dropped. "He'd seriously want you back after everything that's happened?"

His sister shot him a dark look. "He's not a nice guy. If he'd been a nice person, this whole drama wouldn't have happened. Kate had good reasons for running."

He frowned, knowing it was pointless to argue with his fiercely loyal sister.

Kate sank into an armchair and curled her bare feet underneath her. "I'm such an idiot. I can't believe I let things get so out of control."

Megan sighed. "The problem is you never had control over anything. Did you tell Rodney you're leaving?"

She nodded. "He's going to Europe tomorrow as planned with one of his friends. He said he was looking forward to the trip and he wasn't going to waste the tickets."

"Well, that's a relief," Megan said. "He won't be around to bother you for the next few months. Does your mother know?"

She shrugged. "I didn't dare mention my mother but I'm pretty sure he'd been talking to her after she left here. He knew things that he could only have known if he'd spoken with Mom."

Jack stood. "This is all too strange and complicated for me. I'm going to hit the road so I'm back at Snowgum Creek before dark."

Megan nodded. "What's the weather like at home?"

"They're predicting snow tonight and tomorrow. You two had better be careful on the roads."

Kate's mouth curved into a small smile. "We'll be fine. I can't imagine what else could go wrong. I think I've used up my quota of bad luck today."

"Let's hope so," Megan said. "We should probably go to your parents' home now and pack."

"Good idea. I'm going to pack an extra suitcase with

all my precious things. My mother may decide to spring clean while I'm away."

"You're joking," he said. "She'd ditch your stuff because she's angry with you?"

She nodded. "I don't trust her when she's in a mood like this."

"Jack, is it okay if Kate leaves a suitcase in my bedroom at the farm for a few months?"

"Sure. No one else will be using your room." He stared at Kate, his gaze softening. There was more to this story than his sister had let on. Maybe his initial impression of Kate was too harsh?

"Okay, let's go," Kate said. "I want to get this over and done with."

He gathered his gear and followed the girls out of the apartment. He looked forward to a quiet and uneventful drive home to his farm on the southwestern slopes of the Snowy Mountains.

Kate's breath caught in her throat, the magnificent Snowy Mountains dominating the horizon. She down-shifted a gear and the steep road ahead brought them closer to the low-lying clouds. Beside her, Megan lounged back in the passenger seat, flicking through the music playlists in her phone.

Kate inhaled the fresh mountain air, her body starting to relax. "Are we close to your parents' farm?"

"Not long to go now. You'll see the orchards before we reach the house. Jack said Aunt Doris has been baking."

"She's the aunt who made your patchwork quilt?"

Megan nodded. "She lives on the farm and dotes on Jack. She's also a fabulous cook and bakes muffins and cookies to die for."

"Sounds wonderful." Her stomach rumbled. She hadn't eaten much over the past few days.

"Jack said he'd look out for us."

"Good. Six hours of driving is long enough for me. I'm hanging out for afternoon tea."

Megan frowned. "You know, I worry about my brother working too hard. After all the driving to and from Sydney, he has probably been out in the orchards all day yesterday and today catching up on chores. Or, he may have taken a break and gone to church."

Kate lifted a brow. "I don't remember you talking about him attending church."

"Apparently, he started back again recently. I'm not sure why."

"Okay." Her mother attended church every week, mainly to keep up appearances in her social-climbing circles. Kate assumed her mother believed in God, although she didn't pretend to act like a good person the rest of the week.

Megan said, "When Dad retired he handed over the reins to Jack, and the burden of running the farm has well and truly fallen on my brother's shoulders."

"When are your parents coming home?"

"It all depends on Grandpa's health. Although, if I was them I'd spend the next few months enjoying a warm Queensland winter with Grandpa and Grandma."

Kate's revised holiday plans included a stop at the farm with Megan for a few days before Megan borrowed her mother's SUV to drive to the snow. Megan was due to start work as a ski instructor at the snowfields next week. Kate intended on chilling out at the ski resort village with Megan for at least a month before driving back to Sydney. Her savings account held enough money to cover the holiday and she could stay longer if she picked up a job.

She switched on the heater in her car, hoping it still worked. The temperature outdoors dropped as they climbed higher into the mountains. Fluffy, white snow clouds filled the sky. She touched the brake pedal and the car edged sideways.

Megan sighed. "The roads are starting to ice up already."

"I know. I'm taking it slow. At least there's no traffic up here." Rows of apple trees lined both sides of the deserted road.

A movement to the left caught her eye. An enormous gray kangaroo bounded along the side of the road.

"Watch out," Megan said.

Kate hit the brakes and the wheels struck black ice. The car spun on to the far side of the road and a large gum tree loomed ahead. She screamed as the rear of the car slammed into the tree.

Chapter 3

A loud crunch of metal echoed through the orchard. Jack revved the engine of his motorbike and headed toward the road. A herd of kangaroos searched for food and his stomach lurched. Megan and Kate were due to arrive anytime.

The rear end of a white sedan lay perched against a tree. Jack whispered a prayer as he accelerated closer.

His sister climbed out of the passenger seat and waved, a dazed expression clouding her face.

He jumped off the bike and ran into her embrace, relieved she appeared uninjured.

"Not the grand entrance I'd planned," Megan said.

"Are you hurt?"

She shrugged. "I feel fine."

"I've no idea how you escaped unharmed but Kate needs me."

"I'll stay here," she said, kneeling on the ground.

He ran around to the driver's side and stifled a gasp.

Kate's striking blue eyes brimmed with tears, and blood covered a small gash on her forehead above her hairline.

He opened the door and crouched beside Kate. "Are you all right? How does your head feel?"

She wrinkled her brow. "It hurts. My head hit the steering wheel."

"Do you feel dizzy? Is your neck sore?"

She frowned. "I don't know."

"What day is it today?"

"Monday." She met his gaze. "I haven't lost my memory."

He smiled. "I'm glad." He took a closer look at the interior of the car. "Can you move?"

"I think so." Her lower lip trembled.

"Do you feel any tingling in your fingers or toes?"

"No."

He held her gaze. "Okay, I'll help you out of the car. We'll take it slow and please let me know if anything hurts."

She flicked a few loose strands of hair off her pale face, her eyes widening. "Is that blood I can feel?"

He nodded. "But don't panic, it only looks like a minor cut."

She let out a big breath before wriggling out from behind the steering wheel.

"Be careful. The ground is uneven."

She placed her feet on the patchy grass and he cupped her elbows as she rose, fearing she would crumble to the ground like a delicate flower blown in the wind.

She attempted a smile. "My legs feel like jelly."

His gaze searched her face, reluctant to let her go. "You're doing great."

Megan shuffled over beside him and examined the gash on Kate's forehead. "I think it looks nastier than it is. We can clean it up at the house."

"I'll be fine." Kate stood straighter and took a wobbly step back.

His arms fell to his sides. "If you're both okay for a few minutes, I'll ride to the house and bring back the truck."

Megan threw her arms around him. "Thanks for saving the day again."

"No problem. Just don't make it a habit." He winked, swung his jean-clad leg over the motorbike and took off for the farmhouse.

Kate stumbled and leaned back against a sturdy gum tree. She sank to the ground as the enormity of the accident registered in her foggy mind. God must have been watching over them today. She shuddered. What if the front or side of the car had hit the tree?

Jack's warm brown eyes had radiated concern. She couldn't help noticing how his working attire of an old sweater and worn jeans complemented his rugged good looks. Yet again, he'd been cast in the role of her hero and rescuer.

Megan stood beside her. "Wait here and I'll see if I can get our luggage out of the car."

She frowned at the crumpled rear end of her car. "Try folding the backseats forward."

"I'll haul everything out through the cabin." Megan busied herself organizing their luggage to transfer to the truck.

Within minutes a red vehicle powered down the road. Kate struggled to her feet and before long she was seated in the passenger seat beside Megan, riding along a track between rows of apple trees.

The homestead came into view and Kate smiled. The wide veranda surrounding the single-level, sandy-brick house gave the home a welcoming air.

Jack opened the passenger door. His strong hands spanned her waist as he helped her to the ground.

She sucked in a deep breath, the imprint of his hands on her body branding her like a scorching hot iron. Delayed shock must be setting in and messing with her brain.

An elderly lady with a wide smile greeted them on the veranda.

"Welcome, my dear girl. I'm Doris and I think we should call the doctor."

"No, I'm fine."

"We'll take a closer look inside." Doris hugged Megan. "I'm so relieved you're both okay."

Megan frowned. "Kate's car isn't looking too good."

"I'll deal with it tomorrow." Exhaustion overwhelmed Kate. Another problem she needed to resolve.

Jack glanced at his watch. "The local garage should still be open. I can call them and organize a tow truck to move your car there."

"Thanks. I'll dig out my insurance details later."

"Now that's settled," Doris said, "let's go inside and have a nice cup of tea."

Megan and Kate sat down in the dining room and Doris soon brought a tray of hot tea, freshly baked muffins and cookies and put them on the table.

Jack placed a first-aid kit on the table and sat beside Kate, pulling his chair close and examining the cut on her forehead.

Kate inhaled the clean, fresh scent of his aftershave. His work shirt, rolled up at the sleeves, looked like it had seen better days. It fit snugly over his broad shoulders and lean torso.

His fingers, roughened by outdoor work, cupped her cheek as he cleaned the wound.

She closed her eyes, her pulse racing.

"You're lucky the cut is only superficial and in your hairline. You won't have a visible scar or need stitches."

"Thanks."

"No worries. It's the least I can do."

Kate took a shaky sip from her teacup and nibbled on a chocolate chip cookie, but her usual appetite had deserted her. Her life had become a series of disasters.

Jack returned to the orchards and Megan led her to her old bedroom. Exquisite Australian-bush-themed patchwork quilts adorned the twin beds.

"Meg, this quilt is gorgeous."

"An Aunt Doris creation. She has turned her hobby into a thriving business."

Kate stowed her luggage before showering, careful to keep the wound on her head dry. She remembered the care Jack had taken to make sure she didn't need further medical attention, using his first-aid skills to ascertain that she didn't have a concussion. His deep, rich voice had soothed and comforted her. His eyes had a tender look as he patched up her forehead. No wonder Megan adored her brother.

Doris served dinner early and Kate enjoyed the hearty roast lamb and vegetables. She was quiet during the meal, content to listen to the verbal exchange between close family members. Dinner with her mother was formal and conversation stilted. This was so different, so comfortable. Kate almost wasn't listening when Jack mentioned his angst concerning his new accounting software.

"You know, Kate is an absolute whiz at that program," Megan said. "I'm sure she could help you work out the problems."

Kate came back to the present and smiled. "Sure, I'm

happy to help." It was the least she could do, considering Jack's kindness and generosity over the past few days.

"I can boot up the computer after dinner," Jack said.

Doris clicked her tongue. "Jack, dear, don't you think Kate deserves a rest tonight? Can't it wait until tomorrow?"

"I have months of work to catch up and the girls are leaving the day after tomorrow."

"You don't have to do it now," Doris said. "There's no need to rush the poor girl, considering everything she's been through today."

"I really don't mind looking at it tonight," Kate said. She could use a distraction from her problems.

"I need all the help I can get," he said.

Doris frowned. "If you're sure you're up to it, my dear, then we appreciate your assistance."

Kate helped clear the dishes before making her way to the study. The spacious room contained two workstations set up next to a window. She sat in a chair beside Jack and moved the keyboard into a comfortable position.

He smiled. "You have no idea how glad I am to have your help. I've been so busy since Mom and Dad went away that I haven't had a chance to sit down and learn the tricks yet."

Kate searched through the existing files. "Your mother has set everything up. You just need to know what to enter where."

A pile of paper was strewn over the edges of an inbox. "This will take a while to get up-to-date," she said.

"I know. I need to get this mess entered and up-to-date as soon as possible. If Mom could see how out of control things have gotten…" He rubbed his forehead, fatigue lines etching his face. "There aren't enough hours in the day."

"I could make a start on it tomorrow—"

"No way. I'd be toast if Doris discovered you're doing my work."

"Okay, then I'll help by sorting the most recent ones and you can take notes while I process each item."

He stifled a yawn. "Thanks."

"No problem." For the next hour she instructed Jack, not sure how much he absorbed as he fought fatigue. He leaned over her shoulder and they worked side by side, processing each document.

She glanced at the time on the computer screen. "Time to call it a night?"

"Yeah, I'll be up at dawn tomorrow." He held her gaze. "I really appreciate your help tonight."

"I think I owe *you* for all your help over the last few days."

His smiled widened. "No big deal. Things can only get better." He patted her shoulder.

"I hope so." What else could possibly go wrong?

The following morning, after indulging in a delicious cooked breakfast courtesy of Doris, Kate found her insurance documents stuffed in a pocket of her suitcase. She scanned the details and stifled a scream.

There must be a mistake. She reread the figures in the vain hope she'd been incorrect the first time.

If she made a claim, the deductible would wipe out her meager savings.

Her stomach sank. She couldn't afford to go to the snow with Megan. Her credit card was maxed. Rodney had planned to clear the balance and provide her with a monthly allowance, and she hadn't paid attention to the balance until her card was declined yesterday morning.

Her grip tightened on the treacherous insurance documents. No way could she face going back home to her mother. She pictured her mother's gloating face and could just hear her patronizing I-told-you-so speech spurting from her mouth. No, she'd call the insurance company and see what could be arranged. There must be a way to solve this dilemma.

Kate made her phone calls in the kitchen. She slouched on the dining table, her head cradled in her hands, a mug of coffee untouched beside her. Sunlight streamed through the kitchen windows that overlooked the garden, but Kate hardly noticed the beautiful day.

Megan breezed into the kitchen and poured herself a cup of coffee. "What did the garage and insurance company say?"

"The garage said six to eight weeks." She traced a floral pattern on the tablecloth with her index finger.

"That long? Hey, this coffee is lukewarm."

"Yep. They have to wait on parts."

"We can work around this." Megan made a fresh pot of coffee. "I can drive your car back to Sydney in a few months."

"I guess so. The thing is I can't afford to go to the snow and pay for the repairs, too."

Megan lifted a brow. "Honey, that's what insurance is for."

"The deductible is the problem. My credit card is maxed and my savings account isn't in good shape."

"Oh." Megan paused. "I can lend you money—"

"No, Megan. What I need is a job and a place to live."

"You can probably pick up work at the snow."

"Maybe. But what if I get up there and can't find a job?"

Jack strolled into the kitchen. "I can smell fresh coffee."

"Mmm," said Megan. "I'll pour you a cup."

"Thanks." He sat opposite Kate, eyeing her untouched coffee. "Everything okay?"

She met his gaze. "I have car troubles."

"Anything I can do to help? I maintain all my cars."

Megan grinned. "The real reason he's way behind on admin is revealed." She handed Jack his coffee and placed a plate of cookies on the table.

Kate nibbled her lower lip. "The problem is the insurance cost."

"I see." He sipped his coffee. "I guess your skiing holiday is also a problem."

She nodded, dropping her gaze. Admitting her financial ineptitude left a sour taste in her mouth.

Jack finished his second cookie and leaned back in his seat, crossing his arms over his well-defined chest. "What are you going to do?"

She blinked, determined not to reveal how close she was to breaking down. "Go back to Sydney, I guess. Or maybe spend a week with Megan and try to pick up a job at the snow."

Jack sipped his coffee, his silence unsettling.

Kate groaned. "I'm sorry. I shouldn't have said anything. You two don't need to hear my problems…."

"No one could have predicted the accident." He stretched in his seat. "I have an idea."

She lifted her gaze. "I appreciate your concern but I don't feel comfortable borrowing money from you or anyone else."

"What about a job and a place to live? Does that interest you?"

"You can't be serious?"

"After our session in the study last night I came to the conclusion I need to hire someone to do the paperwork if my parents are going to be away for the next few months."

Megan joined them at the table. "What did Mom say?"

"They're spending winter on the Gold Coast and I've

been wondering who I could find locally who is available and has the required skills."

"Jack, this is an excellent idea." Megan swung around in her seat to face Kate. "What do you think? You could still visit me at the snow."

Kate looked at Jack. "I don't know. What would I need to do?"

"I can offer you a set number of hours in the office, and I always need an extra pair of hands in the orchards." He grinned. "Assuming you're not afraid to get your hands dirty. We also have a private guest room with adjoining en-suite facilities. I know Doris would like some female companionship around the house and you could help her with chores."

Kate's mouth opened, but no words came out. This was the last thing she'd expected to hear.

"I can get a contract drawn up, taking into account the cost of board and lodging." He named a generous salary.

She could pay for her car repairs and start clearing her credit-card debt. Not living near a mall for a few months would help her bank balance.

"I need to think about it."

He stood. "There's no rush. My admin nightmare isn't going anywhere."

"Thanks, Jack. I appreciate your offer and I'll get back to you later."

"Sure." He smiled. "I'll be in the orchards if you need me." He left the room and she heard the back door open and close.

She met Megan's gaze. "Should I do this?"

Chapter 4

Kate bit her lower lip. Jack's job offer could be the perfect solution but it would mean living on a farm for a few months. Could she handle it?

Megan smiled. "It's your decision and a better option than returning home to your parents."

"Tell me about it." Borrowing money was out of the question. She didn't want to be beholden to anyone and no bank would lend her money if she didn't have a job.

There was one other option, one she didn't dare voice to Megan. Her diamond engagement ring sat in her suitcase. She could pawn it, although she'd only receive a fraction of its true value. But what about Rodney? Was it fair to keep the ring after everything she'd put him through?

Megan sipped her coffee. "Do you think you could cope, living here for a few months?"

"I'm not afraid of hard work."

"That's not what I mean. Life is very different here

compared to Sydney. The closest mall is a two-hour drive away."

"Well, considering my financial situation, that's probably a good thing."

"And Snowgum Creek is a very small town. Not a lot to do here."

She shrugged. "It's only for a few months. Once I've started clearing my debts and paid for the car repairs, I can line up a job back in Sydney."

Doris strolled into the kitchen, her arms full of groceries. "Can you girls please help me bring a few things in from my car?"

"Sure," Kate said, following Doris and Megan to the adjoining garage.

"Jack offered Kate a job here this morning," Megan said.

"I know." Doris stopped and looked Kate straight in the eye. "What would you like to do? I'd love to have some company around here but you might have better things to do than hang out with an old lady like me."

Kate laughed. "Are you kidding, Doris? You give the old expression 'young at heart' a new meaning."

Would living here be such a hardship? Doris was spritely for her age, and during the short time she'd been here she felt like they could become fast friends. She seemed open-minded and hadn't judged Kate for running away. If anything, she was the exact opposite of her mother.

Kate placed a bag of groceries on the kitchen counter. "Do you think it could work?"

Doris's eyes sparkled. "I sure do. After everything that's happened, it would probably do you good to take it easy and think about what you want to do next. And you'll have lots of thinking time here."

Megan dropped her arm around Kate's shoulders. "After

a few weeks if it's not working out you can still join me at the snow. I really don't think Jack would mind if you left early. Even a few weeks of help will make an enormous difference, catching up on the backlog."

"The problem is the car business is taking up more of his time." Doris shook her head. "I don't know what he's thinking, trying to run both businesses at the same time without help. He'll work himself into an early grave if he's not careful."

Jack did seem very driven. During her brief stay at the farm he'd spent the majority of his time working. Did he ever take time off to enjoy his life?

"Okay, I'll think about it and give Jack an answer before dinner." Megan was leaving tomorrow and she wouldn't let her indecisiveness delay Megan's departure.

Megan smiled. "I'm sure you'll make the right decision."

Doris nodded. "You take all the time you need."

"Thanks," she said. Megan planned to give her a tour of the orchards. Fresh air and sunshine should help clear her head and she'd soon learn if she liked the idea of living on a farm.

Jack finished cleaning up after a long day in the orchards and found the girls playing a game on the large plasma television in the living room. Engrossed in the animated game, they didn't notice him standing in the doorway.

Kate threw her head back and laughed, her long, dark locks cascading down her back. She dropped the controller on the rug. "I give up. You've had more practice than me."

"True." His sister turned and spotted him in the doorway. "Hey, Jack, do you want to take me on?"

He shook his head. "I can never beat you."

Kate stood, tucking her lustrous hair behind her ears. "I've made my decision and I'd like to accept your job offer."

"Great. We need to talk about the details."

Her eyes sparkled. "I need an excuse to avoid being beaten by Megan again."

"You sure do." Megan switched off the game console. "I should finish packing, so I'll leave you two to sort out the details."

"Thanks," Jack said. "I'll brew your favorite coffee."

"Sounds good. Give me half an hour and I'll be done." Megan strolled out of the room.

Jack ran his hand through his hair, still damp from his shower. "I haven't drawn up a contract yet because I wanted to talk first and make sure we're on the same page."

"Okay."

"I'll grab a notebook and set up the coffee machine. We can talk in here."

She sat in a plush armchair, one long jean-clad leg crossed over the other. Her fitted wool pullover sweater accentuated her curves and he decided that now that he was about to become her employer, he'd better focus his attention on her beautiful face.

He fixed their coffee in the kitchen, glad for the diversion. He hadn't thought about it before, but maybe it wasn't such a good idea to have Kate working and living here. He didn't need the distraction of a gorgeous woman, even if she would be here for only a few short months. He'd have to keep firm employer/employee boundaries. How hard would that be?

He returned to the living room, placing a tray on the coffee table.

She grinned. "I'm impressed that you're making the coffee."

"You're forgetting that I have to drive a long way to buy a cup of decent coffee." He passed a steaming mug to her.

"Thanks." Her fingertips touched the back of his hand and a sudden awareness of her close proximity filled his senses. He sat across from her on the sofa and opened his notebook, a much safer option than watching her slightly parted lips as she stirred a teaspoon of sugar into her coffee.

He tapped his pen on the spiral binding. "We can set an hourly rate for office work and helping me in the orchards a few hours each day. You can help Doris around the house in exchange for your board."

She pressed her lips together before answering. "Do you need help in the orchards or are you just offering the extra hours to give me more work?"

He leaned back on the sofa. "Some days I could do with an extra pair of hands. Another option is I could pay you to help with the chauffeur business, although it's weekend work."

"I really don't mind." She sipped her coffee. "This is good coffee."

He smiled. "Thanks."

"I'll do whatever you need, as long as what we agree to is fair for all and Doris is happy with the arrangement."

"Sure. We can play it by ear. Also, I want you to know up front that you'll be a casual employee and can leave anytime. You'll have some flexibility concerning the number of hours and type of work you do each week. And if you're not happy, I don't have a problem with you taking off to stay with Megan or moving back home."

She nodded. "That sounds more than fair. I think I can handle a few months of country living."

"Okay." He stretched out his hand. "It's a deal. Welcome aboard."

She shook his hand and he held her gaze. Moments later he reluctantly let go of her smooth hand, wondering how she'd cope with getting her nails chipped and hands dirty from outdoor work.

"Jack, I really appreciate this opportunity. Thank you."

"No worries." He grinned. "You may not be thanking me after you learn I'm a hard taskmaster."

Her blue eyes twinkled. "I'm up for the challenge."

She looked determined, and he was glad he'd taken the plunge and given her a chance. Even if she only lasted two weeks, it was two weeks less work he'd have to catch up on later. If she stayed, the next few months were going to be interesting.

Kate stood beside Jack on the veranda, waving to Megan as she drove away in a cloud of dust. It was a done deal. She'd be working on the farm for the next few months and spending a lot of time with the handsome man standing beside her.

Jack smiled. "What are your plans for today?"

"Since I start work tomorrow, I thought I'd take it easy, maybe read a book or watch a movie."

"Sounds fun."

"Yeah. And the not-so-fun thing I need to do today is call my father."

He raised an eyebrow. "Does he know about your change of plans?"

"Not yet, but he will soon." She dreaded making the phone call, and had put off contacting her father until Megan had left and her decision was final.

"Okay. Well, feel free to use the house phone. Sometimes the cell phone connection can be dodgy."

"Thanks, but I'll try my cell phone first." She still had

a lot of credit on it and should be able to top it up after she received her first paycheck.

"Doris will be back after lunch and I'll be in the orchards," Jack said as he stepped off the veranda and strode out toward the sheds. He walked with an air of confidence, as if he was sure of himself and his place in the world. He had direction in his life, a plan to build up the farm and car business. He'd recently purchased a vintage white Bentley to add to his collection but her favorite car was the maroon Cadillac. Although maroon wasn't a traditional bridal car color, he hired it out for various events and functions.

In her bedroom she located her purse and switched on her phone. Seven messages, and five of those were from her parents.

She listened to the third message from her mother and cringed. Right now she didn't have the patience or the energy to deal with her mother and her issues.

She selected her father's number and he answered on the second ring.

"Hi, Dad. How's things?"

"Katie, I'm so happy to hear from you. Are you well? Did you have a safe trip?"

"Sort of," she said.

"What do you mean? Are you okay?"

"Yeah, I'm fine but my car is in bad shape." She told him about the car accident.

"You poor thing. I worry about you driving on the mountain roads at this time of year. Is Megan okay?"

"Yes, she left for the snow this morning."

"Where are you? I thought you were going to the snow with her."

"Um, I changed my mind. Megan's brother offered me a job for a few months."

"A job." He paused. "Why do you need a job? Where will you live?"

"Dad, slow down. I have a little cash-flow problem as a result of the accident and I can't afford to go to the snow with Megan."

"How much do you need? I can put the money in your account today."

"No, Dad." Her voice softened. "I appreciate your offer but I need to stand on my own two feet and handle this myself."

"What type of work will you be doing?"

"Accounts. Similar to my last job. And I'll be living here with Jack and his Aunt Doris."

"Hmm. This Jack fellow is the one with the Cadillac, isn't he?"

"Yep, Megan's brother. And he's been very kind and is drawing up a generous employment contract."

"Your mother is going to have a fit."

"She'll get over it."

"I don't think so. Honey, is there any chance you can call her sometime? She's worried about you."

Yeah, right. If only it was that simple. "I know, Dad, but I need some space and some time to sort myself out."

"My offer of a loan still stands. Wouldn't you prefer to hit the ski slopes with Megan instead of working on a farm?"

"Dad, I know you mean well but you won't change my mind." For too long she'd taken the easy option, doing what other people wanted to keep them happy. Look at the mess she'd created by not standing up to her mother concerning Rodney.

"Are you sure? The money's there if you need it."

"Thanks, Dad, but this time I'm going to do it myself." She also didn't want her father to discover how irresponsible she'd been with her finances. Nor did she want her mother to learn her father had lent her money. He'd keep it between them but her mother had a way of finding things out.

"Okay, Katie, I'll support your decision. Hard work never did anyone any harm. If this is what you really want…"

"It is, Dad. It will give me the time I need to work out what I want to do next."

"Sounds like a good plan. But there's something else you need to know."

"Oh, you're sounding awfully serious."

"Your mother is still convinced that you should marry Rodney when he returns from Europe."

"You must be kidding! After everything that's happened…"

He sighed. "I know. I can't quite work out her obsession but she's beside herself over the way you ran from the church and claims the social shame is nearly killing her."

"For goodness' sake, people will talk for a while and then it will be ancient history. I'm not the first bride to get cold feet at the last minute."

"As I said, I don't understand why it's such a big deal. To be honest, I never really took to Rodney and it's probably for the best that you ended it."

"Dad, I'm sorry that I didn't speak up earlier and break the engagement. I tried talking to Mom but…"

"She wasn't listening. I remember all too well. Look, you need to talk to her soon, help her see reason over this situation. She won't listen to me."

She wouldn't listen to Kate, either. "All right. I'll call her eventually." She needed to be feeling strong and sure of herself before she made that particular phone call.

"Okay, take care. And message me so I know everything is fine with you."

"Sure, Dad. Thanks for understanding."

"No worries. We'll talk soon."

She ended the call and ran her fingers through her wavy hair. Why couldn't her mother be reasonable? Why was she so fixated on her marrying Rodney?

Strings of guilt tugged at her heart. She loved her mother and wanted to please her, but this time her mom was asking too much. When would her mother let go and realize she never intended to marry Rodney, no matter how much her mother pushed and begged and pleaded her case?

Chapter 5

Kate shut down the computer and stretched out her legs under the desk. She glanced over the neat pile of paper in the inbox. Each day the pile became smaller and a sense of accomplishment filled her.

Over the past few weeks she'd found her life revolved around the farm. There were more varieties of apples than she'd imagined and she discovered Jack liked to muck around grafting branches, seeing if he could come up with a new strain that would be the next big trend.

She smiled. It had only taken her a week to tidy and organize the office. She ploughed through her work each day, finishing midafternoon to help either Doris or Jack. Doris appreciated her help around the house because it gave her more time to work on her knitting and quilting business.

Today it was Jack's turn to enlist her services. She layered on extra clothing and pulled her beanie down over her ears, allowing her hair to flow loose beneath it. The wind had a winter bite despite the warmth from the afternoon sun. She wrapped her scarf around her neck, pulled on her outdoor boots and trudged down to the sheds in search of Jack.

She was now familiar with the layout of the orchards, often spending an hour in the morning walking and running through the maze of trees. She found the crisp mountain air invigorating, a stark contrast to her usual indoor workout at the gym.

Jack was an early riser, and he waved in greeting as he rode by on one of his assortment of toys. Sometimes she hitched a brief ride on the back of the tractor. Other times he flew by on either his motorbike or the four-wheeler. The past few days he'd been hanging high in the air above her, pruning the top branches using the cherry picker.

She approached the sheds and spotted Jack nearby. He drove the cherry picker over to the four-wheeler. A trailer was attached to the back of the bike.

"Hey, there," he said. "It's your turn to ride the bike."

Kate eyed the trailer, calculating the width of the track between the rows of trees. "Including the trailer?"

He nodded. "You'll just need to go slower than your usual breakneck speed."

She bent her head to hide the deep shade of red spreading up her neck. Her fast runs on the bike along the perimeter fences had not escaped his notice. "Okay, then. I'll follow behind you."

She maneuvered the bike along the tracks to the far orchards, careful to slow as she descended the steep hill. Turning corners with the trailer was tricky but before long she made the turns with ease. Dense, white clouds began to build overhead and the light breeze blowing around her face had a different feel.

Jack worked his way up and down each row while she

gathered the felled branches to bundle up in the trailer. Over the next couple of hours she made four trips back to the shed. The noise of the cherry picker plus the fact that Jack was fifteen feet above her made conversation between them impossible. Kate enjoyed laboring in the orchards, her mind given the space to ponder and process her thoughts.

There was nothing like working outdoors to give her some perspective. Jack was a fair boss. He expected her to work hard but he hadn't been harsh when she'd messed up once or twice. She admired his strong work ethic and his determination to get the job done.

Following Jack's instructions, she parked the bike and trailer in one of the sheds, and waited outside for Jack to catch up. Low-lying clouds filled the sky, blocking out the sun.

He pulled up beside her and lowered the open cabin platform to ground level.

He smiled. "Thanks for your help today."

"I don't mind working outdoors."

"How about you jump in beside me and I'll show you how to operate this baby?"

"Okay." The cherry picker was one piece of machinery she'd yet to explore. She stepped onto the tiny platform and Jack stood behind her, close enough for her to feel the warmth emanating from him through her layers of clothing.

He stood on a foot pedal and began their ascent high into the air. "The view through the valleys is incredible on a clear day."

"I'm sure it is." She surveyed the distant scenery, the usual jitters she experienced from being so far off the ground not bothering her. Jack's broad arm loosely encircled one side of her as he demonstrated how to steer and drive the cherry picker forward and back. His steady voice evoked feelings of safety and security. At that moment she realized she trusted him in a way she trusted few others. A keen sense of awareness shot through her and she savored this small pocket of time together.

She gasped as snowflakes drifted down toward the trees above her. "Jack, it's snowing."

"We need to pack up and get indoors before it gets heavier."

She sighed. "I've never seen snow falling before."

"It's something special." He pressed the pedal to lower them back down again.

"I've been to the snow a few times but it has never actually snowed while I was there. I guess I've seen a lot of manmade snow instead of the real thing."

"Wait until you wake up tomorrow and see snow everywhere, including all over the trees in the orchards."

"How cool." She stepped onto the ground and spun around to face him. "Thanks for showing me this."

His wide smile lit up his eyes. "My pleasure. I thought you'd like it."

She returned his smile and the connection between them intensified. Was it possible she was developing more than a friendship with Jack? This thing they had happening between them had moved up to a new level.

Jack was her boss and she'd be leaving in a few months. But a part of her cherished lingering thoughts about him and now questioned her premise that a relationship between them was impossible.

She helped Jack stow the last of the farm machinery in the sheds and trekked with him to the house. The snowflakes melted as they hit the ground. She shook out her beanie, scarf and jacket on the small porch before entering the warm homestead.

Jack sat on the bench beside her and they untied and removed their outdoor boots in tandem.

He turned to face her. "If the snows set in, I'll be working indoors for a few days. I may even take some time off."

"There are a few things in the office I need you to look over at some stage."

"There are also a number of things I need to do in Sunny Ridge."

She smiled. "When are you thinking of going?"

"Maybe Wednesday next week, assuming you don't mind spending part of your day off with your boss?"

"As a matter of fact, I wouldn't mind wandering around a shopping mall for a few hours." She missed living close to a mall.

"I want to leave early since it's a two-hour drive each way. I should get all my errands done by lunchtime. We could meet at the mall for lunch and I'll show you some of the sites afterward?"

"Sounds like a good plan." She walked ahead of him to the kitchen, switching on the kettle to make tea.

The phone rang and Jack ducked out to the living room. Kate busied herself making a pot of tea and searching the cupboard for treats. Dinner was still a few hours away and working outdoors gave her an appetite. She found homemade shortbread and organized afternoon tea for two. Doris was due back later but she suspected the snow would bring her home early. She glanced out the window. Dense, white flakes were building up on the ground, creating a sea of snow.

Jack ended his call and joined her for afternoon tea. He turned to the window. "What do you think?"

"It's beautiful, and it doesn't feel as cold as I thought it would."

"The air changes and becomes very still just before it

snows. If you're here long enough you'll learn to read the signs."

She nodded, wondering how many snow showers she'd see over the next few months. She'd made the decision to stay on the farm and stick it out. The office work was relaxing without having pressing deadlines and a manager looking over her shoulder.

She missed her gym and her favorite coffee haunt, but the peace and quiet was a balm to her injured heart.

He poured a mug of tea. "I also have a favor to ask."

"Sure." She owed Jack for giving her a job and a roof over her head. How could she say no?

"I was just talking to Josh, my car-business partner. We have a job coming up in a few weeks and I need an extra pair of hands on site."

Her grip tightened on the handle of her mug. "A wedding?"

"Yes. The local pastor's daughter is getting married. She has a large bridal party and the groom comes from a big family."

She dropped her gaze and stared out the window. "What do you need me to do?"

"Not a lot. The photos will be taken at the church and the adjoining village green in town."

Her stomach lurched. Vivid memories rose to the surface and filled her mind. She hadn't been near a church since she ran away from Rodney. Nor had she seen a wedding party up close and personal since that fateful day.

He frowned. "I understand you may have reservations—"

"No, I'll be okay." She pasted a bright smile on her face. Somehow she'd cope with the memories that being around a wedding would generate inside her head.

"Are you sure?"

She nodded. "I can't avoid weddings forever."

"Doris usually helps me on the few occasions we need an extra pair of hands. Doris is a guest at the wedding and the reception venue is at least an hour's drive from the church. Lindi, Josh's wife, is struggling with morning sickness, and being around food isn't a good thing for her right now."

"I understand. So you'll need me to organize food and drinks beforehand."

"Yes. Doris said she'd do it but she needs time to get ready and I want her to enjoy the day instead of working."

She nodded.

And I'll need help at the venue serving food and drinks. I'd do it myself except there will be thirty people at the photography session and Josh and I need to be available for the bridal party. She has four bridesmaids."

"Wow. You will be busy." She could do it. She was determined to face her fears and become stronger after knowing she could be near a church without succumbing to a panic attack.

She tilted her head to the side. "Um, I do have one question. How will I get there, since my car is out of action?"

"I'll drive you." He sipped his tea and grabbed another shortbread biscuit. "The bride lives up the road from the church. I'll drop you off at the church early then make my way to the bride's home."

"Okay." At least she wouldn't need to face her fear of winter driving. Motorbikes on the farm she could handle, but the thought of negotiating mountain roads, possibly snow-covered mountain roads, sent a chill through her body.

"Do you have something to wear?"

"I think so. I packed a white shirt and black tailored pants."

He smiled. "Perfect. Please make sure you wear your hair up. Doris will do the shopping and on the day of the wedding she can run through the food-handling regulations."

"I worked in a café a few years ago and I have an idea of the requirements."

"Good. Keep track of the hours you work and I'll make sure you're paid the following week." He named a fair hourly rate.

"Okay, it's a deal." The extra money would come in handy and help her clear her credit-card debt faster. She sucked in a deep breath. She wasn't going to panic about being confronted with her worst nightmare. Weddings are fun. People are happy at weddings. She'd put on her happy face and do her best to enjoy the day.

"Oh, I forgot to mention I'll need you to babysit the cars while Josh and I watch the wedding ceremony in the church. We both know the families of the bride and groom."

"No worries." Relief flowed through her now that she had a rock-solid excuse to avoid stepping foot inside the church. Unless it rained and she was forced to seek shelter indoors. No, she was going to think positive and assume the bride would get her ideal sunny and clear winter day.

He drained his cup. "Josh and Lindi are coming over next weekend for a barbecue. Lindi and Megan were friends at school and Lindi's looking forward to meeting you." He paused. "Unless you have other plans?"

She shook her head. She'd only been here a few weeks and had visited town once with Doris. The farm was her safe cocoon from the world and she was happy to hide away and have time to contemplate her future.

Maybe it was time to spread her wings and broaden her horizons. She couldn't hide away from the world forever. "A barbecue sounds fun."

Butterflies leaped in her stomach. She had two weeks to gather her resources and face her fears. In some ways it felt like her wedding day was just a bad dream. Coming face-to-face with another wedding would make her experiences all too real.

Guilt nagged at her soul. Could Rodney and her mother forgive her for what she had done? More important, could she forgive herself for leaving him at the altar?

Chapter 6

Kate applied lipstick and checked her appearance in the bathroom mirror. Jack waited in the garage, preparing for their drive to Sunny Ridge.

What a difference fresh air and lower stress levels made to her face. Her complexion glowed and she'd lost the frown lines between her eyebrows.

She entered the garage to find Jack dressed in business clothes. He cut a dashing figure in his single-breasted suit and she was glad she wore a fancy top and long skirt with her favorite jacket.

Jack smiled. "You're looking great today."

"Thanks. And you're looking pretty good yourself. Do you have an important meeting this morning?"

He nodded. "The local growers association is lobbying to increase our export markets. I learned a while ago that we're more successful in negotiations if we dress like our urban counterparts."

"Sounds good." After witnessing Jack standing up to her mother, she imagined he'd be a tough negotiator and would achieve his desired result.

The drive to Sunny Ridge passed quickly. Snow lay on the side of the road, although it was melting fast under the morning sun. The stores were just opening when Jack dropped her off at the mall.

Kate checked the mall directory, pleased to find a couple of her favorite stores located in the mall. With three hours to fill and numerous sales taking place throughout the mall, she should be able to find a few bargains.

Three hours later Kate rode the escalator down to the food court level, her hands full of bags containing clothing, shoes and accessories.

Jack waited at a table outside a café, his head buried in a newspaper. For a moment she wondered what life would be like if he was her husband, waiting for her to complete her retail therapy indulgence and join him for lunch.

She shook her head, unable to forget she'd run away from a husband and a European honeymoon. She could have been skiing in the Swiss Alps instead of shopping on a budget in a small-town mall. She straightened her shoulders. She'd learned the hard way that she didn't need a rich husband to make her happy.

Jack glanced at the lunch menu on the blackboard. After a successful morning of negotiations he was ready for lunch. He looked around and spotted Kate heading his way. He waved and stood, pulling out a chair for her.

"Thanks." She lined up her shopping bags beside a terracotta pot next to their table before dropping into the seat opposite him.

He eyed the bags. "I see you've had a busy morning."

She smiled. "I love to shop. What can I say?"

"You're the quintessential city girl." The number of bags she had managed to collect in such a short time astounded him. It confirmed his belief that she was a high-maintenance girl who liked the good things in life. And yet her willingness to get her hands dirty and work in the orchards didn't quite fit that image.

She shrugged her shoulders and glanced over the menu. "I grew up in Sydney and spent my teenage years hanging out at either the mall or the beach. This is my comfort zone whereas the orchards are yours."

"My life on the farm is a far cry from your glamorous life in Sydney."

She sighed. "It's not all fun and excitement. There's a lot to be said for communing with nature and chilling out away from the hectic pace of city life."

"But before long you'd become bored with farm life. The majority of girls I grew up with left as soon as they could." A hint of disappointment tinged his voice.

"Can you blame them for chasing career opportunities that aren't available in small towns?"

"Not really. Look at Megan. She only lives in one place for about six months before she's bored and searching for her next exciting opportunity."

"Sometimes it's hard to believe you two are related because you're so different."

"You mean she's the exciting one and I'm the dull one who works all the time."

"Not at all." Her eyes sparkled. "I'm sure you do exciting things every so often."

A waiter arrived at their table to take their order. Kate selected the fish of the day with salad and he chose the rib eye fillet steak with a medley of vegetables.

As each day passed he realized how much he liked

having Kate around. She brought fun and adventure to the usual humdrum routine that had become his life.

"Jack, I completely forgot to ask. How did your meeting go?"

He smiled. "Exceptionally well, and it was a win-win situation for everyone."

"Excellent. What are your plans for this afternoon?"

"There's a well-known garden maze not far from here, with a colonial-style teahouse attached." Last week he'd discovered they both shared a common interest in board games and puzzles.

"Sounds fun. I haven't visited a maze since I was a child."

"It's a long time since I've been to this one but from what I remember it's quite challenging." He used to race Megan through the maze, laughing as they ran into each other, lost and disoriented. Eventually, they would join forces and make it to the finish, only to find their parents had beaten them out and were waiting for them at the teahouse.

The waiter served their food and they chatted over lunch, covering a range of topics. He found Kate an entertaining companion and at times forgot she was his employee, not his lunch date.

After lunch he helped carry her shopping bags back to his SUV, catching the many admiring male glances sent her way. Kate seemed oblivious to the attention. A part of him liked the idea of being her date and wished the circumstances were different. He would enjoy spending time with her while it lasted but he was under no illusion that they could ever share a future together.

Within ten minutes they reached the entry to the garden maze. The manicured hedge was over twelve feet high and a quaint cottage with wide, covered verandas looked down over the maze.

He paid the entry fee for both of them, squashing her protests that since he'd paid for lunch she should pay this time. His logic was that she'd proven herself to be an excellent employee and deserved to be spoiled today.

They reached the first decision point in the maze and she turned to face him.

"How long is it going to take us to reach the end?"

He grinned. "That all depends on how many dead ends we go down."

"What's the secret? There must be some clues to help us."

"From what I remember the end of the maze is right next to the teahouse. We must end up heading toward the roof, which we'll be able to see when we're close to the end."

She glanced up at the cloudless blue sky. "I guess the direction of the sun will also help us?"

He nodded. "Pay attention to where it is now. The teahouse is on the western side of the maze, which makes it easier at this time of day."

"Let's do it." She checked the time on her watch and grabbed hold of his hand, leading him to the fork in the maze on the left side.

"Hey, don't I get a say in this?" he asked.

"We could take turns, swapping over when one of us reaches a dead end?"

"That works for me." Her hand fitted neatly into his, like two pieces in a jigsaw puzzle. He was reluctant to let go, hoping it was part of the game.

Jack discovered he outlasted her in the patience stakes. Frustration radiated on her face when they reached one dead end after another.

She slumped down on one of the many benches located

in the maze, throwing her hands into the air. "I give up. I'm sure we've passed this spot at least three times."

He sat beside her, suppressing the urge to laugh. "The good news is we've eliminated the section in front of us. My guess is the end is not far behind us because the sun is heading that way."

"I hope so. I'm ready for afternoon tea. After all this walking I can afford to splurge on something laden in calories."

He laughed, curbing the desire to brush back a wayward lock of hair from her forehead. "How about you relax and let me find our way out of here."

"Okay, I concede your sense of direction is superior to mine. But I'm still the reigning Scrabble queen."

"Sure." He neglected to mention that his extra six inches of height had allowed him to glimpse the teahouse roof behind them. He needed every advantage he could find when trying to outwit her. Plus the thought of being her knight in shining armor and rescuing her again held some appeal.

Kate packed the last of the lunch dishes into the dishwasher. Lindi stood at the sink, cleaning up the greasy barbecue utensils.

"Thanks for your help," Kate said.

Lindi smiled. "No worries. I'm glad I had a chance to meet you. The boys will be ages tinkering with the cars so we may as well sit down and chat."

"Are you feeling okay?"

"I start feeling better as the day goes on. Just don't peel a banana in front of me or open a tin of tuna."

She giggled. "That I can manage. I'll make a pot of tea."

"Sounds good." Lindi pulled out a chair at the dining table beside the kitchen counter. "You know, I really appreciate you volunteering to help at the wedding next weekend. I was the backup plan but, as you've discovered, I'm not having a good relationship with food at the moment."

"Totally understandable." She'd enjoyed listening to Lindi talk about her pregnancy.

"And I'm glad I can attend the wedding ceremony. I went to school with the bride and groom."

"I guess that's the norm in a country town, where everyone seems to know everyone else." She organized a tray for the tea and waited for the water to boil.

"You better believe it. There are no secrets in a small town."

"I'm fast learning this." She poured the boiling water into a floral, ceramic teapot and carried the tray to the dining table.

"Are you feeling okay about being around a wedding?"

She slipped into a seat opposite Lindi and lowered her gaze. How did Lindi know about her wedding fiasco? "Did Jack tell you?"

"No, Doris accidentally let something slip when she asked me to help in your place and I connected the dots." She ran her fingers through her short, blond hair. "Doris felt bad about saying something and she was concerned you'd find the whole wedding thing confronting. I promise I won't breathe a word."

She nodded. "I appreciate that, although I'm only here for a few months so I guess it doesn't matter if a few people learn the truth." She had assumed Doris, of all people, would try to respect her confidentiality. But Doris did like to talk a lot and she liked knowing all the local gossip. At least Doris had good intentions. Kate really didn't want the whole town to discover she was a runaway bride.

"To tell you the truth, Doris is very aware that people are going to be watching Jack, not you."

She raised an eyebrow. "Why?"

"He hasn't said anything?"

"Nope. Is there something I should know?"

"The town grapevine is working overtime this week. I think it's better for you to hear this now rather than have some nosy gossip asking you questions."

She widened her eyes. "What? Are people talking about me living out here with Jack and Doris?" Did the townsfolk think she and Jack were in a relationship?

"Yes and no. You've kept a low profile, so naturally people are curious. And everyone will be at the wedding."

"But nothing is going on between me and Jack. I mean, it's only three weeks since I left Sydney…"

"You and I know that, but everyone else will be speculating. Anyway, that's not going to be the biggest topic of conversation."

"Oh. What else could be bigger?" She couldn't imagine she'd done anything that could be perceived as scandalous in the past few weeks, with the exception of leaving her fiancé at the altar. And if no one knew about that, then what else could Lindi mean?

"Have you known Megan for long?"

"We met quite a few years ago in Sydney. Why?"

"Did she talk about Jack, mention any ex-girlfriends?"

Kate drew her brows together. "I did once meet his long-time girlfriend at a party. I think she's the one who moved away to Sydney. What was her name? Emily?"

"Amy."

"Yes, that's right. It was Amy." She remembered Megan telling her that he'd taken the split pretty hard.

Lindi nodded. "They dated in high school, split up when he went to university in Sydney then got back together for a year or so before she moved to Sydney."

"The story is starting to come back to me. When I met her they'd just got back together and Jack was in his last year at university." Kate'd had a crush on Jack, knowing nothing could ever come of it, and recalled how he'd doted on the beautiful, blonde woman. They had seemed so in love....

"He was serious about her and then, out of the blue, she announced she had a new job in Sydney and was breaking up with him."

Kate poured tea into two teacups. "What's this got to do with the wedding?"

"Amy's younger sister is the bride."

"Oh." She sucked in a deep breath. She wasn't going to be the only one next weekend struggling with issues from the past.

"And Jack is driving the bridesmaid's car, since the bride wanted her bridesmaids to ride in the Cadillac."

She added milk to the cups and passed one to Lindi. "And I'm assuming Amy is in the bridal party."

"The matron of honor."

"She's married."

"Rumor has it she met a rich doctor not long after she moved to Sydney and they married soon after."

Wow. She had no idea what a minefield this wedding was going to be for both her and Jack. She sipped her tea. "And is Jack okay? I mean, he's not acting like anything's wrong. And it's, like, at least three years since all this happened."

Lindi stirred sugar into her tea. "This will be the first time Jack has seen Amy since she left him. She got married in Sydney and occasionally visits her family. I haven't seen her in years."

"I guess this puts things in a different light."

"The gossips will be watching Jack and Amy to see how they cope being around each other." Lindi sipped her tea. "Everyone knows things didn't end well and that Amy ran off."

"What can I do?"

Lindi sighed. "I don't usually talk about stuff like this, but Josh and I care about Jack and we didn't want you to hear about this from one of the gossips who will be hanging around."

"Surely the bride's family will close ranks and not talk."

"Absolutely, but the groom comes from a large family. And a couple of well-known local gossips are his close relatives. We just wanted you to have a heads-up so you won't accidentally walk into a difficult situation."

"Thanks." Maybe she should call Megan this week and see what she thought about the situation. She owed Jack, and if she could make his life easier at the wedding then she'd do it. Thankfully, she hadn't taken the easy way out and said no to working for him at the wedding. It was going to be an interesting weekend.

Chapter 7

Kate stowed the food and drinks for the wedding in the back of the Cadillac before slipping into the front seat. Memories of the last time she traveled in this car deluged her and she closed her eyes, willing them to disappear. This time she was dressed in a white collared shirt and black tailored pants, ready to serve the family and bridal party during the photo session.

Jack swung into the driver's seat and grinned. "All set."

She nodded. "I triple-checked the list and I don't think I've forgotten anything."

"Sounds good. Let's get this show on the road." The Cadillac roared to life and she gripped the door handle as they drove down the long drive and onto the mountain road.

He shot her a concerned look. "Are you okay?"

"Yep."

"Then why are you about to dig a hole in the leather upholstery with your fingernails?"

"No, I'm not." She moved her hands to her lap, clenching her teeth to try and keep her hands in a relaxed grip.

He grunted and kept his gaze glued to the road.

Her stomach twisted. They approached the tree at the site of her car accident and she stared at her feet, not wanting to remember the horrible moment when her car connected with the sturdy trunk. It had to get easier. She had driven vehicles on the farm but hadn't been on this stretch of road since the accident.

She sucked in a deep breath and opened her eyes. Jack remained silent but he must have noticed the tension in her body. Thankful he didn't comment, she stretched in her seat and settled back on the soft leather.

Jack hummed along to a song on the local radio station. She kept her gaze averted, taking in the passing scenery.

They reached the main street of Snowgum Creek and he drove into the church car park.

"Will you be all right here by yourself? I should have lent you the SUV—"

"No, it's okay and I don't mind waiting." The sun shone bright in the clear sky and she looked forward to wandering through the gardens adjoining the church grounds.

"All right." He smiled. "I'll be back with the bridesmaids in around half an hour."

She waved goodbye then stood still, studying the church. A quaint sandstone structure with pretty stained-glass windows, it was surrounded by a well-kept lawn and a circular drive at the front.

Her heart tightened in her chest. Was it only four weeks since she was last, albeit briefly, in a church building? So much had changed and she was still no closer to working out what she wanted to do with her life. Treading water on the farm was a great temporary solution but she had to return to the real world eventually.

Rodney would be in Italy now, Milan, to be exact, if she remembered the itinerary she'd studied weeks ago. She shivered. Was he still furious with her? Could a few months away help him realize she'd stopped both of them from making a massive mistake? She hoped he'd return from Europe with a new perspective and the knowledge that they needed to go their separate ways and move on.

She sighed. She couldn't love Rodney the way a woman should love her husband. Goodness knows she'd tried, especially after her mother was so intent on making them a good match. But the spark just wasn't there for Kate. He had seemed oblivious to her reticence, wanting her to take steps in their relationship that made her feel uncomfortable.

If only she could turn back the clock and refuse his romantic wedding proposal in a chic Sydney restaurant. She'd been blinded by his wealth and the lifestyle he could give her, ignoring, to her detriment, the other warning signs about his character. If there was one lesson she'd learned from the sorry mess, it was to not allow money to cloud her judgment. And to never again let her mother push her in a direction that she knew, deep down, was totally wrong for her.

Before long a crowd gathered outside the church and Doris came over to talk to her.

"Doris, you look wonderful," she said.

"Thank you, my dear. You're looking very professional."

She smiled. "I'm here to do a job."

Doris glanced at her gold wristwatch. "The bride should be arriving any minute."

A distinctive rumbling engine pierced the chatter and the Cadillac came into view, followed by a white Jaguar.

Jack stepped out of the car and rolled a red carpet from the rear door to the entrance of the church.

"Doris, I'd better discreetly make my way to the cars."

"Good idea. I'm going to head inside to find my seat. My friend Betty is saving one for me."

"Have fun," Kate said before strolling toward the cars. The bride sat in the Jaguar, smiling at the cameras flashing around her.

Kate bit her lower lip, glad she was wearing sunglasses to hide the moisture building behind her eyes. She clenched her fists. She could do this. Smile and hope no one could see the inner turmoil rolling through her like waves pounding the shore.

She hovered behind the crowd around the Jaguar, blending in with the guests. The bride alighted from the car and one of her bridesmaids, a petite blonde wearing a gorgeous pale blue silk dress, adjusted the train behind her.

The blonde looked like Amy. She found Jack in the crowd, standing to the side, his gaze fixed on the blonde as she moved ahead to join the other bridesmaids and flower girl. Sunglasses shaded his eyes and his expression gave nothing away.

He looked in her direction and tilted his head, indicating she should join him. Kate skirted behind the crowd moving into the church and stood between Jack and Josh as the bride entered the church.

She turned to Jack. "How's everything going?"

"Fine. We're going to move the cars to the edge of the parking lot next to the village green and then slip into the back of the church."

"Okay."

"The service will only run for about half an hour. It would be great if you could set up the food and drinks table in twenty minutes on the grassy area beside the cars."

"No problem." She followed the Cadillac down the

circular drive and into the dirt car park, glad to be moving farther away from the church.

Jack handed her the car keys before walking back to the church with Josh. A bench seat under a shady tree beckoned her and she leaned back on the wooden seat, listening to the pretty crimson rosella birds chirping in the park. No one else was around, and she assumed the entire town had piled into the church to watch the wedding. She was thankful that Jack had understood her lack of desire to watch the nuptials take place.

Before long the church bells pealed and the bridal party appeared on the front steps of the church, surrounded by well-wishers. Kate had everything ready on the fold-out table, more than happy to watch the photo session from a distance. After a number of group photos were taken outside the church, the crowd started to disperse and a group of ladies broke away, heading in Kate's direction.

She pasted a big smile on her face, determined to keep her emotions at bay and act like a professional as she served the drinks.

A plump, middle-aged lady stayed by the table, nibbling on the Camembert and biscuits. "This cheese is good. I don't buy it myself because I could eat an entire wedge in one sitting."

Kate nodded and maintained her polite smile, thankful she had two more wedges stashed in the cooler bag beside the table. "I'm glad you're enjoying it."

"Yes." She popped another biscuit in her mouth. "Did you see the wedding?"

She shook her head and lined up a row of plastic glasses.

"That's a shame. The groom is my nephew and his bride looks stunning in her dress from a posh Sydney boutique. You're from Sydney, aren't you?"

"Yes." She opened a bottle of sparkling apple juice.

"I love weddings and I haven't missed a wedding in this town in five years."

"Wow, that's an impressive record."

"As you've probably discovered, everybody knows everyone here and our young folk often come home to get married."

"That's nice." She placed more glasses on her serving tray.

"There's something about weddings that always puts a smile on my face. That special moment when they exchange their vows and say I do is marvelous. I lost my husband to cancer a few years back but I remember our wedding as clearly as if it happened yesterday."

"I'm sorry to hear that."

"It's okay, dear. We didn't have all the fancy technology back in the day to record my wedding ceremony but I love watching wedding movies and have a big collection."

"Lots of good movies feature weddings."

"I know. I watched a runaway bride movie last night and I can't understand how a bride can run out on her own wedding. It makes for a good story but fancy wasting a beautiful dress and all the arrangements that go with the wedding."

Kate's hand tensed on the bottle and she lowered her gaze. "I guess she had her reasons."

The lady huffed and sipped her drink. "I don't understand how a decent woman could even contemplate the idea of wasting thousands of dollars and inconveniencing people."

Kate blinked rapidly, wishing she was wearing sunglasses. She turned her back on the woman to rearrange the food. "Who knows why people do what they do?"

"It's selfish, if you ask me. And imagine being in the groom's shoes, watching his beloved running away. And the poor mother of the bride, having to cope with pitying looks from family and friends. The public humiliation would be awful."

She looked up and the bride and groom appeared from behind the church, surrounded by guests and posing for photos under an old gum tree.

Kate straightened her spine, trying to keep the tone of her voice even. "It's been nice chatting but I need to start distributing these drinks to the guests."

"Of course, dear. Please don't let me hold you up." She swiped another wedge of cheese on a biscuit and headed into the crowd surrounding the bride.

Kate sucked in a steadying breath and picked up the tray of drinks. Talk of runaway brides had sent her heart racing into overdrive. Did this woman know her history or was it a coincidence? She walked across the lawn, handing out drinks as she went before returning to the table to refill her tray. The lady's attitude suggested she'd be up front and tell the truth if she did know what had happened four weeks ago.

But she couldn't deny the truth in the woman's words. Her decision to run from the church had hurt Rodney and her mother. And her mother wasn't being a drama queen concerning the pitying looks and everything else her father had mentioned.

She sighed, guilt pricking her conscience. It was time she took responsibility for her decision and called her mother. She couldn't put off the difficult confrontation any longer. Despite everything, she loved her mother and had never planned to intentionally hurt her. Could her mom forgive her for humiliating her?

After refilling her tray she headed over to the bridal party. Josh had already served drinks to them and she stood to the side, watching the bride and groom pose for the camera.

Jack held a platter of cheese and biscuits and worked his way through the gathering. The blonde bridesmaid grabbed Jack's arm and whispered something in his ear.

Kate froze, keeping her smile intact as Amy's hand lingered on Jack's arm.

Jack said something to Josh and handed over the cheese platter. He wandered off to the edge of the crowd with Amy, disappearing behind a large gum tree.

She collected empty glasses and returned to the table to refill the few remaining ones. Josh met her at the table.

"How's everything going?" he asked.

"Good, I think." She tucked a strand of hair behind her ear.

"You're doing great and the guests are starting to leave now for the reception venue."

"Thanks. It looks like my job is nearly done."

"Yes, and thanks again for helping us out. Lindi really appreciates you filling in for her."

"No problem. I'll clear away the remaining glasses and start packing up."

"Good idea. I have a platter and drinks put aside for the bridal party. They're planning to spend at least another half hour here for photos. Jack's taking care of something and then he'll take you back to the farm."

She nodded. Her gaze roamed in the direction of the large gum trees, searching for Jack. She found him and Amy having an animated conversation. Amy grabbed hold of his hand and Kate let out a sigh before dragging her attention back to the task at hand.

It's not like she was jealous, or had any right to be jealous. Then why did she feel like telling Amy to back off and leave Jack alone?

Chapter 8

The leaves crunched under Jack's shoes as he shortened his stride to let Amy catch up.

Amy. The girl he'd once thought he was destined to marry. The girl he hadn't seen since she left him three years ago. And now she wanted to talk with him.

He looked down on her blonde head, still a foot shorter than he was, despite her heels. "So what do you want to talk about?"

She paused, glancing up to meet his steady gaze. "Why don't we talk behind that clump of trees? Do you remember when we were kids and we used to play hide-and-seek here?"

He nodded. "Seems like a very long time ago. Where's your husband?"

She spun around and tilted her head. "Over there."

A man dressed in an expensive tailored suit stood apart from the crowd, holding a phone close to his ear. "I thought he'd be with you, mingling with your family."

She dropped her gaze and her lower lip trembled. "Yeah, well my husband is anything but predictable."

"I heard he's a big-city doctor."

"You heard right. He has a busy practice and likes the good life. A simple country wedding doesn't rate highly on his social calendar."

"Interesting. I wouldn't have guessed that you'd marry a party boy."

Amy strolled to a bench behind the trees. "He works hard and is entitled to enjoy his downtime."

He frowned. "You know, if I were him I wouldn't be happy to see my wife wander off with her ex."

"He's not you, Jack." She brushed her fingertips over the wooden bench before perching on the edge.

He sat beside her. "Are you okay?"

"Of course. I'm happy to see my sister married. Wasn't the service beautiful?"

"Your father did a good job. I had wondered if he was going to give your sister away instead of performing the ceremony."

"Mom was more than happy to walk my little sister down the aisle."

He leaned back in the seat and crossed his arms over his chest. "Amy, what's up?"

Her smile faltered. "You know, Jack, you're one of the good guys and I don't think I appreciated that enough when we were together."

His jaw fell slack. "What are you saying?"

"I'm sorry." She leaned forward in her seat, resting her head in her hands. "I shouldn't have dumped you and moved away without giving you a chance to think things through."

"What things? You made your feelings crystal clear the last time I saw you."

She met his gaze. "If only you would have considered moving to Sydney. You lived there for three years and it wasn't that bad—"

"No." He stood. "My life is here, on the farm. There's nothing you or anyone else can do to change my mind."

"But Jack—"

"You always had unrealistic expectations. I can't believe you really thought I might seriously consider a permanent move to Sydney. You know I've always dreamed of running the family orchards. And for the record, I hated living in the city."

Her eyes widened. "Oh, you know how much I hated living here."

"I never understood that, since you were born and bred here."

"Sometimes the grass isn't always greener."

He returned to the bench and sat next to her. "Do you regret leaving?"

She shook her head. "I regret hurting you but it was something I had to do. Can you forgive me?"

He nodded. "I've moved on and you've made a new life for yourself. I wish you all the best."

"Thanks." A smile hovered over her lips. "It's about time you found yourself a good woman. What's the deal with Kate?"

"Kate? What do you know about Kate?"

"The town gossips are speculating all sorts of things. I know she's Megan's best friend and that she's living with you on the farm."

"She's my employee, that's all. And she's doing me a favor by catching up the farm admin while my parents are away."

"I can't help but wonder…"

"You're impossible and I don't owe you any explanations—"

She raised her hands. "Hey, take it easy. I only asked a question and, having known you for a long time, I find your answer very revealing."

"Don't you go adding fuel to the fire. We're friends. That's all."

She shrugged. "You can deny it all you want, but I've seen the way you've been looking at Kate. And I'm probably not the only one who's noticed."

He leaped to his feet. "Speaking of Kate, I need to drive her back to the farm before I drive the bridal party to the reception." He checked his watch. "I better get moving."

"Sure." She stood. "Thanks for listening."

"And don't be a stranger. You know where I live when you next visit town."

She frowned. "It probably won't be for a while."

He walked with her back to the photo shoot, grinning when the bride called Amy over for more photos. He understood Amy's desire to live in Sydney. But he couldn't help questioning how happy she was with her husband, who was still talking on his phone.

It took a special woman who could cope with life on the land without all the conveniences of city living. He found Kate waiting beside the Cadillac, and he couldn't imagine she would be content being a farmer's wife. She appeared to enjoy her current life but it was only temporary and the novelty would wear off soon.

Kate packed away the last empty platter and closed the boot of the Cadillac. She let out a big sigh. It was over and she'd survived being in close proximity to a wedding. She'd kept it together and hadn't burst into tears or done anything embarrassing.

As she'd tidied up, she couldn't help but overhear the chatter among guests concerning Jack and Amy wandering off together. The big topic of conversation was speculation regarding the state of Amy's marriage. Her immaculately groomed husband was deemed arrogant and too self-important to mingle with Amy's family.

Both families considered Amy's husband's behavior rude, since he'd grabbed a drink and spent the rest of the time with his ear glued to his phone, oblivious to the fact that his wife had disappeared with her ex-boyfriend.

Jack strode toward the Cadillac and pulled his car keys out of his pocket. "We need to get moving."

Kate smiled. "I have everything packed up and ready to go."

"Thanks." Jack opened the passenger door of the Cadillac for her. "I appreciate your help today. You did a good job."

"No problem." She slid into the car and fastened her seat belt. "I'm more than happy to help."

He revved the engine and steered the Cadillac down the circular gravel drive to the road. "Everything has gone smoothly, so far."

"I left a supply of food and drink with Josh for the bridal party."

"Thanks for that. He said they have at least another half hour of photos to go before they head to the reception."

"Okay. I'm glad dropping me home won't make you late."

"You know, you could have borrowed one of the cars."

Kate pressed her lips together. "I should have my own car back soon."

He tapped his fingers on the steering wheel. "I get it. I know you're avoiding driving after the accident."

She frowned. "I just need a little time, that's all. I don't mind driving around the farm."

"It's good practice."

She squirmed, changing the subject. "The bride looked beautiful and the bridesmaid dresses were a gorgeous color."

"Everyone is happy with the day so far. No dramas, well, maybe with the exception of Amy."

"Why is everyone talking about her? When you two were chatting, all the family could talk about was Amy and her husband."

"She usually comes alone when she visits her family. This is only the second time he has been to Snowgum Creek."

"Really? How long have they been married?"

"Couple of years. He's a busy doctor in Sydney and can't get away. Even today Amy said he had work phone calls to field after the ceremony."

"That explains a lot."

"Oh?"

"She seems like a nice girl. I remember meeting her once, years ago in Sydney when I'd first met Megan and you were at university."

He smiled. "That's right. Amy and I got back together not long before I moved back home. It's interesting talking to Amy again. She has everything she wanted and doesn't look happy."

Kate turned to look at Jack. "What do you mean?"

"She has a wealthy husband, lives in a big house in the eastern suburbs of Sydney and is living her dream of studying full-time at university. What more could she want?"

She laughed. "You're serious, aren't you?"

"She has the life she said she always wanted."

Kate read between the lines and realized he meant the

life he couldn't give her. If only he understood how flawed his thinking was in this area. Not all women were obsessed with hooking a wealthy husband who could provide them with a life of luxury.

She examined her fingernails, looking a little worse for wear after a few weeks of working in the orchards. Maybe she could stretch her budget and invest in a professional manicure soon. "Money doesn't make people happy."

"Being flat broke and starving never made anyone happy, either."

"Yes, but having bucketloads of money is no guarantee of happiness. Sure, it helps to not have to struggle financially, but it's no guarantee of a perfect life."

"What makes you so sure?"

"I walked away from a wealthy fiancé and it was the best decision I ever made in my life."

"And you have no regrets?"

She shook her head.

"Even now, when you're doing menial work around the orchards?"

"I don't mind working in the orchards. The fresh air and slower pace of life is a refreshing change. Rodney inherited a lot of money and lives in a North Shore mansion. He could live off investments for the rest of his life and never need to work. But all his money was never going to make me happy."

"I don't know many women who would walk away from that kind of money."

"You haven't met Rodney. And my parents have been in a good financial position for most of their marriage, and it certainly hasn't helped make their marriage any happier. Their relationship has been rocky for as long as I can remember."

He frowned before turning into the drive leading up to

the house. "I hope Amy is okay. Things didn't end well between us but I wished her well and I hope she has a nice life with her rich doctor husband."

"Relationships take a lot of work on both sides. I'm sure it will work out."

He nodded. "I hope you're right."

Jack woke early the next morning. Last night he'd promised Doris he would drive her to church. He straightened the collar of his shirt and made his way to the kitchen. He had time for toast and coffee before they left.

Kate slouched at the table, nursing a mug of coffee. A half-full coffeepot sat beside her empty cereal bowl.

Her eyes widened. "Morning."

He smiled. "You're up early. Would you like toast?"

"No, thanks, are you going somewhere?"

"Church."

"Really?"

He nodded. "Doris and I are leaving in half an hour."

"Okay." Her finger traced the rim of her coffee mug. "Do you go to church often?"

"I'd like to go more regularly. Now that you're doing the admin, I'm hoping to take Sundays off work."

"Good idea. It's important to take time out from work."

"Yes." He placed two slices of bread in the toaster. "My family tells me I work too much."

She lifted a brow. "Do you agree?"

He opened the fridge, locating butter and homemade strawberry jam. "Maybe. I think it's important to be prepared for hard times when your livelihood is dependent on the weather and other things you can't control."

"Is that why you started the car-hire business?"

He turned to face her, meeting her steady gaze. "It's one reason. I love tinkering with old cars and decided to turn an expensive hobby into a business." Amy had been opposed to his starting the car business, claiming he'd have no time to spend with her. In hindsight, she was right and his spare time had been consumed by the cars. Now he only played touch football at the park in town when he didn't have work to do in the orchards or a Saturday wedding scheduled.

She sipped her coffee. "Would you like a cup? It should still be hot."

"Thanks. That would be great." He located a mug in the cupboard and passed it to Kate.

The toast popped up and he spread butter and jam on the slices before joining Kate at the table. He added milk and sugar to his coffee, inhaling the aroma before sampling a taste.

She tucked her hair behind her ears. "So you don't go to church every week because you don't have the time to spare."

He raised an eyebrow. "Kind of. I mean, there's no rule that says you have to attend services every Sunday." In recent months he had started praying more often and reading his Bible.

"I used to go to church all the time when I was at school. Now I only go at Christmas and Easter."

"What happened?"

"My friend got pregnant in her last year at school and my church rejected her."

"That's not how a church community is supposed to work."

She shrugged. "They didn't want her around because her pregnancy was embarrassing. Her wealthy parents were very involved in the church and didn't cope well with her situation. She ended up keeping the baby and being helped out by the kind people at Rosewood."

"Rosewood?"

She pressed her lips together, her eyes glassy. "It's a North Shore mansion that's leased by a Sydney charity that helps teen moms." She sighed. "The people at Rosewood saved my friend's life."

"I'm sorry your church experiences were negative." He couldn't imagine the caring people at Snowgum Creek Community Church being cold and judgmental toward a young girl in need.

"It's not your fault."

He drew in a deep breath. "Would you like to visit my church this morning?"

Chapter 9

Kate widened her eyes, unprepared for Jack's question. "Um, I was planning to finish reading my book this morning."

He smiled. "No worries. You're welcome to tag along to church anytime if you change your mind."

"Sure, but I don't know if God would want to see me at church."

"Why?" His brows drew together. "I mean, I'm not sure why you think God wouldn't want you at church."

She sucked in a deep breath. "Well, for starters I'm a runaway bride. I've messed up big time and I know I'm not good enough for God."

Doris walked into the kitchen and switched on the kettle. "Kate, dear, no one is good enough for God."

Jack nodded. "I know I'm definitely not, but He still loves me despite my failings."

"I'm confused," she said. "Don't you have to follow all the rules in the Bible?"

"We're all human and make mistakes," Doris said. "It's impossible for us to live perfect lives and be fully obedient to God."

She sipped her coffee. "My mother has always told me that I need to do things to please God, to make sure I'll get to heaven."

Doris frowned. "Do you go to the same church as your mother?"

"Yes, but I usually only go to keep her happy." She explained her church attendance history to Doris and Jack.

Doris made a cup of tea and joined them at the table. "Your mother hasn't given you an accurate description of what the Bible teaches."

"I totally agree," Jack said.

She held his warm gaze. "Which part has she got wrong?"

He cleared his throat. "I suspect she may not fully understand God's love and forgiveness through Jesus."

"Oh, I know the Christmas and Easter stories." She had listened to countless sermons over the years explaining the gospel message.

"It's having faith that determines whether or not we go to heaven, rather than good works," Doris said.

She lifted a brow. "But don't you need both?" She had faith and believed, but wasn't it logical that good people who followed the rules went to heaven? And bad people like her had to hope they were good enough in God's eyes to get into heaven.

Doris's eyes softened. "You've asked a complex question that I'd love to talk about now, if I only had more time."

He glanced at his watch. "We need to leave in ten minutes."

Doris drank the remainder of her tea. "We can talk more over lunch."

She nodded. "I don't want to hold you up and make you late."

"I can try to answer your questions," Doris said. "But you can go straight to the source."

"You mean the Bible?"

"Yes. You'll find answers to your questions in God's word." Doris stood and walked over to a nearby bookshelf. She picked up a worn, brown, leather-bound book from the shelf and handed it to Kate.

She ran her fingers over the embossed leather front cover. The Bible looked old and well used. "I don't know where to start."

"One of the gospels, maybe Mark, but I also recommend the book of Romans. The early chapters will help answer your last question."

"Do you mind if I borrow it to read in my room?"

"Of course not." Doris smiled and carried her teacup to the kitchen sink. "I own more than one Bible."

Jack nodded. "She has half a dozen floating around the house."

"Okay, thanks."

He snatched his car keys off the counter. "We'll be back after eleven, depending on how long Doris wants to stay for morning tea."

Jack and Doris left the kitchen and she opened the Bible, checking out the list of books on the index page. She found the page number for Romans and flicked through the delicate pages, locating chapter one. After brewing a new pot of coffee, she curled up on the sofa and started reading. She was curious to learn the truth.

Two days later, Kate stacked the last of the dinner plates in the dishwasher. Jack stood in front of the sink, soap suds bubbling over his capable hands as he scrubbed a saucepan.

"Here, I'll dry that one with a tea towel," she said.

"Thanks." He handed over the saucepan and let the water drain out of the sink.

Kate smiled. They'd fallen into a nighttime routine. Doris cooked most evenings and Kate helped Jack clean up the kitchen after dinner. They chatted as they worked, each night taking it in turns to wash up the saucepans in the sink and load the dishwasher.

"Okay, I'm done." She spread the tea towel over the warm railing in front of the cooling oven.

"Are there any good movies on television tonight?"

She shook her head. "Tuesday is a slow night and there's not much on."

"How about a DVD? Or a game of cards or Scrabble?" His eyes twinkled and the corners of his full lips tipped upward.

"Not tonight." She sighed. "I need to call my mother before I chicken out and put it off for another day."

He nodded. "It's probably better you make the call tonight. Then you might stop fretting about the situation."

"Maybe." She tilted her head to the side. "Anyway, how do you know I've been worrying about making the call?"

He reached out and trailed his index finger between her brows. "Because you have frown lines here that won't go away."

She met his gaze and looked deep into his tawny-brown eyes.

"And," he continued. "You know it's the right thing to do, even though it won't be an easy conversation."

"I guess you're right." She rolled her shoulders and leaned back against the kitchen counter. "The longer I leave it, the worse I feel."

He grinned. "You'll be fine. It's a six-hour drive from Sydney so you have time to escape if it doesn't go well."

"Don't say things like that. I can't imagine my mother driving here to visit. She prefers to travel by air to exotic locations."

He chuckled. "Are you saying my hometown isn't good enough for your mother?" A teasing smile hovered at the corners of his mouth.

"Yes, and for this reason you should be thankful. You know, I'm really sorry she yelled at you at Megan's apartment."

"Don't worry about it. I understand she was stressed. Now, you'd better stop procrastinating and go make that phone call."

She nodded. "Wish me luck."

"Absolutely, and unfortunately I think you'll need it. I'll pray it goes well."

"Thanks." Even God probably didn't have the power to sway her mother's opinion in her favor. But Jack's prayers couldn't hurt and God might listen to him.

She left the kitchen and made her way to her bedroom where she kept her phone.

Jack hadn't commented on Rodney and she wondered if he had issues with her reckless behavior. Did Jack side with Rodney? Did he think she was irresponsible for running out of the church and leaving Rodney at the altar?

She frowned. Jack had been in Rodney's shoes when the girl he'd loved left him for a new life in Sydney. Amy had relocated with no warning and hadn't given him an opportunity to win her back. It was possible Jack's sympathies lay with Rodney, although Jack didn't know the full story explaining why Kate ran.

In fact, no one knew about the secret she'd discovered a few days before the wedding. She hadn't even told Megan, her best friend in the entire world. And Megan would probably rip into Rodney if she knew the truth.

If only her mother had listened to her when she'd told her she had serious doubts about going ahead with the wedding. If only Kate had been more open with Megan about what was bothering her. But it was too late now to change what had happened.

She squared her shoulders and settled onto the edge of her bed, her phone beside her. The moment of truth had come.

With shaky fingers, she speed-dialed her mother's phone.

Her mother answered on the third ring. "Oh, Kate, I'm so happy to hear from you. Are you okay?"

"Yes, I'm fine."

"I've missed you and I worry about you." Her mother paused. "Your father told me you'd contacted him. Why didn't you call me sooner?"

Stung by the bitter edge in her mother's voice, she took a deep breath. "I needed time to think. I didn't mean to hurt you."

"Well, at least you called me now." Her mom's voice lightened. "I've been keeping busy since you've been gone. The church fair was last week and we're organizing a fashion parade to raise money for the children's hospital."

"I'm glad you're doing well."

"And your father is well, and he improved his golf handicap last weekend."

"That's nice." She started to relax, falling back into the familiar and comfortable relationship she'd previously shared with her mother. A relationship she missed. Moisture started to build behind her eyes and she blinked rapidly to keep it at bay.

"But Kate, dear, what I want to know is when you're coming home."

Home. Her hand tensed around the phone handset. "Not for a while. I'm happy here at the moment."

"You can't be serious!"

"I am, indeed. It's nice to have a break in the country." She didn't want to return to the family home. When she moved back to Sydney, she'd lease an apartment somewhere.

"But Rodney will be back soon. He sent me a lovely postcard from Venice and he mentioned how he misses you. He wants to see you when he returns home."

"Really? I find that rather surprising," Kate said.

"You know he loves you and you're so lucky he's prepared to work things out and give you a second chance."

Second chance. Why? What didn't he understand about her running away from their wedding? How could he even think she'd want to get back together with him?

"I'm not interested in working things out with Rodney."

"How can you say this?" Her voice raised another octave. "It's obvious you two are destined to be together."

Only her mother could twist the facts and come to such a conclusion. She sucked in a steadying breath. "This time you're not going to get your wish."

"My wish? I know that deep down this is what you really want. When you've had time to calm down and think, you'll swallow your pride and realize you made a big mistake in jilting Rodney."

"I don't think so."

"Nonsense. He's handsome, rich, everything a girl could want."

"Mom, please listen to me. I'm not going to change my mind. Marrying Rodney would be a big mistake—"

"Kate, stop it. You're upsetting me with this silly talk."

"Why are you so determined to see me marry Rodney? Why won't you listen to me?"

"Because you love him and he'd make a good husband."

"I don't love him."

"I know you're upset and confused right now but in time you'll realize I'm right."

"Let me spell it out to you. Rodney cannot make me happy. I'm not in love with him."

Her mother's shrill voice rang through the handset. "You can't believe this. You must marry him, otherwise my life will be ruined."

"Mom, what on earth are you talking about?"

"It's just that…" She paused, sounding like she was fighting back tears. "Look, I love you and I only want what's best for you."

Kate stood and paced the length of the room. Why couldn't her mother listen to her and be considerate to her needs and wants instead of trying to run her life?

"Okay, Mom, if you really love me you'll give me the freedom to make my own decisions and live with the consequences, good or bad."

Her mother huffed. "I'm very disappointed by your attitude and lack of respect. You're not the daughter I raised."

The phone line went dead. Kate bit her lip, frustrated that her mother hadn't given her an opportunity to respond.

What was wrong with her mother? Was she having a midlife crisis or some kind of emotional meltdown? The social shame would diminish over time as people forgot about the runaway bride incident. Why was her mother desperate for her to marry Rodney?

She walked into the adjoining bathroom and blew her nose. Tears threatened at the corners of her eyes but she held them in check. Maybe Megan could provide her with answers to explain her mother's seemingly irrational behavior.

Pain stabbed at her heart as she acknowledged her mother's rejection. If she wanted her love and acceptance then she'd have to submit to her mother's will and marry Rodney. How was that fair or loving?

The big question remained. Why was her mother prepared to lose her relationship with her only child over this issue?

Chapter 10

Kate handed over two vanilla cupcakes with pink frosting to the girls at the head of the queue. For the past few hours she'd been selling the cutest cupcakes to the townsfolk gathered for the Saturday afternoon touch football match. The church ladies were raising money for the local school.

Doris tapped her on the shoulder. "You can finish up now."

"Are you sure? This queue isn't going away."

"More helpers have arrived and the barbecue is about to start."

"Okay." She spun around to find Jack standing at the front of the line.

She lifted a brow. "Hey, you're early."

"But I'm right on time to take you to lunch." He grinned. "Can I please have a chocolate cupcake? Which one would you like? Let me guess, chocolate."

She tipped her head to the side. "How did you know?"

His eyes twinkled. "I've been paying attention."

Really? She didn't know he'd noted her likes and dislikes. Her pulse raced as she packaged the cakes and collected his money.

"Thanks," Jack said. "Let's go."

She said goodbye to the ladies at the stall and walked beside Jack, heading toward the barbecue on the other side of the park. The winter sun warmed her skin and brought a smile to her lips.

Jack held the cakes carefully, negotiating the uneven ground. "Josh and Lindi have set up a picnic table under the trees."

"Sounds nice. Are you hungry?"

"Always. The line up for the barbecue is this way."

After leaving their cakes in a safe place on their picnic table, he guided her toward the marquees. Smoke twirled in the air from the large outdoor grills. The tall gum trees nearby provided shade and a long table had been set up, complete with bread, sauces and salad.

"Mmm, this smells great." Her stomach rumbled in anticipation of a delicious lunch.

They joined Josh and Lindi in the lunch queue.

Lindi smiled. "Did you have fun at the cake stall?"

She nodded. "I can't believe how many cakes we sold in such a short time." The church ladies were welcoming and had appreciated her assistance.

Jack's hand lightly cupped her elbow as they moved forward in the line. "It's all for a good cause. I hear the school may lose more funding next year."

Josh grabbed hold of Lindi's hand. "My good wife skipped out on helping with the cake stall."

Lindi nodded. "But I'm finally having an okay food day. Too much sugar doesn't agree with me at the moment."

She turned to Kate. "Did you buy a cupcake? They always taste good."

She shook her head. "I didn't have time."

"But I did, and she chose well." Jack smiled. "She has exceptional taste in selecting chocolate, although I'd already guessed her choice."

Lindi pulled her straw hat lower over her face. "It seems like you two have had a lot of time to learn each other's preferences."

"I guess so," she said. "I'm ahead in the great Scrabble challenge."

"But not by far." Jack shuffled forward with her toward the front of the line.

"Speaking of chocolate," Josh said, "Kate, did you know chocolate is the prize today for the winning touch footy team?"

"No, I wasn't aware," she said.

Jack paid the volunteer behind the table, and she filled her plate with chicken, salad and a bread roll.

Kate waited for the others and they walked together to their picnic table set up under a gum tree.

Josh pulled out a chair for Lindi and smiled. "So Kate, you have to play on my team this afternoon because we will win the chocolate."

Jack shook his head. "You're dead wrong. My team will win today."

Kate sliced up her marinated chicken breast and savored the delicious tandoori flavor. "I haven't played touch footy in ages."

Jack raised an eyebrow. "You've played before?" He bit into his steak sandwich, ketchup and onions oozing out the side.

Kate passed over a napkin. "When I was at school, and I had a lot more energy back then than I do now."

"I don't know. I've seen you running pretty fast through the orchards," Jack said.

Lindi giggled. "Kate, you've dobbed yourself in now. Since your name was drawn in Josh's ballot, he's going to make you play, especially knowing you're a runner and have played before."

"How did my name end up in the ballot?"

Jack shrugged. "Equal opportunity. Everyone in town is eligible to play."

She narrowed her eyes. "It seems like someone was hoping to draw my name." She turned to Josh. "It looks like you're stuck with me."

Josh nodded. "You've got that right. And we're going to win."

She met Jack's noncommittal gaze, his eyes hooded and giving nothing away. Was Jack disappointed that she wasn't selected for his team?

After stacking their plates, Kate helped Jack clean up the table while Lindi rested with Josh.

They dumped the trash and walked back to their picnic table.

Jack smiled. "Are you ready for the big match this afternoon?"

Her gaze roamed over the playing field where the teens were finishing up their match. "It should be lots of fun, and you were right about one thing."

"Which is?"

"The ground is muddy and I'm not wearing shoes with the best grip."

He glanced at her pristine running shoes, still looking like they were brand-new. "I hate to tell you this, but your shoes won't look so great by the end of the match. At least dirt and mud is easy to clean off."

She grinned. "I hope so."

Not long after they packed away their gear in Jack's truck, the teens finished their match and Kate headed across the park with Jack and Josh. Trash bins with flags were arranged to designate the playing area. She mentally recapped the basic rules of the game. The ball must be passed backward and kept in the field of play, although the ball could be kicked forward. A touch to any part of the body stopped the play. The team had six chances to reach the scoring line before a changeover occurred, and the ball had to be placed on the ground over the line to score points.

She followed Josh and their team huddled together. He briefed the team on tactics and she paid close attention. Thankfully, she was allocated her preference of an attacking rather than defending position.

The match commenced with a big cheer from the crowd on the sidelines. There seemed to be an equal number of girls on each team. The ground was slippery and before long her hands and legs were covered in mud. At the half-time break her team was behind by one point and the competition between the two teams had heated up.

She nearly scored a couple of times. Her last attempt failed when she had a clear run to the line and couldn't hold on to the slippery ball. Meanwhile, Jack had already scored at least three times for his team.

The call went out that there was two minutes to go until full time. The score was even and one more touchdown would put her team in the lead. Josh passed the ball to her and she caught it clean, seeing her chance for a touchdown by running straight down the sideline.

She pumped her legs hard and her breathing constricted her lungs. Only twenty feet to go and the winning points were hers. Out of the corner of her eye she spotted Jack chasing after her, intent on running her down. She upped her speed, her muscles burning for more energy. Jack was not going to stop her this time.

With three feet to go, she dived for the line. She closed her eyes as mud splashed all over her face and body. Jack's hand enclosed her lower leg but he was too late.

She rolled over to find Jack lying next to her, covered from head to foot in mud.

"Congratulations, and look at the mess you've got us both into."

"But I had to dive for the line so you wouldn't catch me."

He laughed. "You dived just as I reached out to touch your back. By the time I got hold of your leg you were over the line."

"Thank goodness." She blinked, raising her muddy hand to block the sun. Did mud cover her whole face? Ugh, she must look a fright.

He propped up on an elbow and trailed his index finger along her cheekbone, his gaze intense. "And you've given yourself a muddy facial for good measure."

She wrinkled her nose, her gaze captured by his brilliant eyes. "I'd prefer a spa facial, thanks very much."

His smile widened. "I think you look cute, covered from head to toe in mud."

She sat up, wiping muddy strands of hair back off her face. Her teammates ran over and she greeted them with high fives as they congratulated her.

Josh gave her the biggest high five. "Well done. With one minute to go, I think we're safely in the lead." He turned to Jack. "Better luck next time, my friend."

Jack stood, mud dripping off his clothing. "I'm calling it a day."

"Me, too," she said. "You can keep playing but I want a hot shower to clean off all this mud."

Jack extended a muddy hand to help her up off the ground. She dreaded looking in a mirror right now. But it had been worth it. The others took their positions back on the field while she walked beside Jack to his truck.

She groaned. "I don't think I've ever been covered in this much dirt in my life."

"You'll get used to it, especially if you repeat today's competitive tactics."

"My mother would have a fit if she saw me now."

"You can always send her a photo or a copy of the match on DVD. I'm looking forward to seeing the replay of your dramatic dive in the mud."

"I guess I'll see the humor in this situation one day."

He grinned. "Your match-winning finale will be the talk of the town for quite some time."

"Great, just what I need." She glanced into the truck's side mirror and suppressed a squeal. She nearly didn't recognize herself. Jack was right. She had no need to indulge in a facial anytime soon.

She hopped up into the truck next to Jack, careful to sit on an old towel he had draped over her seat. He still managed to look good, even covered in mud. In contrast, she was looking her absolute worst. She had redefined the definition of a bad hair day.

The next morning, Kate ran her fingers through her blow-dried hair as she headed to the kitchen. She reached the entrance, inhaling the invigorating aroma of freshly brewed coffee.

Jack leaned against the kitchen bench, holding a steaming mug. "Morning. You're up early."

"Yes, I thought I'd join you and Doris at church this morning."

He smiled. "Sounds good. Would you like toast?"

"Thanks." She poured coffee into a mug and added milk. "How much time do I have?"

"Half an hour, although I haven't seen Doris this morning."

"Maybe she ate an early breakfast?"

He shook his head. "I've been awake since six, and she hasn't made her usual morning cup of tea."

"I hope she's okay." Doris was healthy for her age, but she suffered from asthma and worried about bronchitis and pneumonia during the winter months.

"She may have slept in after staying up late to finish the quilt."

"True." She sipped her coffee, liking the strong flavor. Doris hated saying no to new orders, and often took on projects with tight deadlines.

"I'm glad you've decided to come along to church this morning."

She nodded. "The church ladies were really sweet yesterday, and invited me to the service." She'd spent a number of hours reading the Bible, and Doris had been willing to answer her questions. But she also needed to conquer her fears by visiting a church.

"They're genuine and welcoming," he said.

"Yes, and very different from my mother's church friends."

He raised an eyebrow. "In what way?"

"Mom's friends do a lot of charity work and good things in the community, but they aren't warm or approachable. I wouldn't feel comfortable talking to them in the same way I can talk to Doris."

"It's good you can talk with my aunt."

"Yes, she's very patient."

The toast popped up, and he passed over a plate with two slices.

She smeared peanut butter on her toast and nibbled on a crust.

Doris entered the kitchen, wearing an old, pink sweat suit.

Kate frowned. "Are you okay?"

Doris slumped into a seat at the nearby table. "I have a touch of asthma, so I thought I'd better stay home and rest."

Jack nodded. "I'll make your usual breakfast."

"Yes, please. You are a dear to look after me."

"No problem." He finished eating his last slice of toast, and pulled a box of Doris's favorite cereal out of the pantry.

Kate placed her plate and mug on the table, and slid into a seat beside Doris. "Will you be okay staying here by yourself?"

Doris nodded. "I'm glad you're going to church with Jack."

She swallowed hard. What would everyone else think when she turned up at church for the first time with Jack?

Chapter 11

Kate stepped out of Jack's SUV in the Snowgum Creek Community Church parking lot. The winter sun warmed her face as she surveyed the sandstone church. People of all ages milled around outside and filed into the building through a door at the back of the church.

Jack stood beside her, catching her gaze. "Are you ready?"

She cleared her throat, burying her sweaty hands in her coat pockets. "I guess so." She resisted the urge to run, determined to face her fears. The ladies she'd met yesterday were friendly, and no one knew her runaway bride history.

He activated the lock on the SUV. "I assume you'd prefer to sit at the back."

"Yep." She fell into step beside him, a brisk breeze whipping her hair across her face. She tucked the wayward strands behind her ears as they approached the church.

A number of people greeted Jack and she smiled as he

made the introductions. She ignored their inquisitive looks, instead diverting their attention by mentioning Doris was unwell.

Minutes later she stood on the threshold of the church, bad memories washing over her. She shivered and drew in a deep breath.

Jack frowned. "Are you cold? The heaters should be on."

Her smile wavered. "I'm fine."

"You sure?"

She nodded.

"Okay." He greeted the usher, accepting a news sheet as he entered the church.

She walked inside with him, her gaze drawn to the exquisite stained-glass windows lit up by the morning sun. Colorful rays of light filtered across the sanctuary, creating a soft and welcoming glow. She exhaled and her muscles relaxed as she sat beside Jack in the second to last row from the back. Her cozy seat in the corner partially hid her from the congregation moving forward along the center aisle.

She wriggled out of her coat, her hands clammy from clenching her fists tight in her pockets.

Jack turned in his seat. "The service should be starting any minute. Do you want to stay after for morning tea?"

"I don't know." She pressed her lips together. Even in her corner position, she could sense speculation surrounding her presence with Jack was creating a minor stir. Aware of the guarded looks and quiet whispers, she shrank back in her seat, not wanting to draw attention to herself.

"You can let me know after the service. I want to stop at the bakery on the way home to buy something for lunch."

"Good idea."

He sank back in his seat. "Would you like to go for a drive this afternoon?"

Her heart swelled. "Sounds fun, as long as Doris is fine on her own."

The pastor spoke into the microphone. He welcomed everyone to the service, and she stood with Jack for the opening song.

She attempted to sing the unfamiliar words until she realized Jack was silent. She glanced at his strong profile, his brows drawn together. Maybe he wasn't comfortable being in church, either, despite knowing everyone in the congregation.

The song ended and she sat down, glad it was over. She had never liked singing in public, even as a child.

Jack lounged back in his seat, his arm resting behind the back of her chair.

Was he trying to provide more fuel for the gossips? She sat forward, resting her elbows on her knees and bending her head. *God, I'm trying really hard to enjoy the service but it's not working. Are You sure I belong here?*

The row behind was empty, and the church was half-full. She listened to the announcements for upcoming activities. In a few weeks she'd be leaving Snowgum Creek, ready to resume her old life back in Sydney.

A Bible rested in a pocket behind the seat in front of her. She flicked through the pages, locating the relevant verses for the Bible readings. She kept the Bible open in her lap as the pastor began his sermon.

Her eyes remained glued to the front, transfixed by his words. Did God really love her in the same way a devoted father unconditionally loved his children?

Moisture pricked her eyes as she remembered her father's response to her running from the church. He had accepted her decision, and tried to understand why she had left Rodney. He didn't condemn her, or attempt to make her feel guilty.

In contrast, her mother had displayed the full extent of her anger and disapproval, and had done her best to force her to change her mind. Weeks later, she still held a grudge and withheld her conditional love.

A verse in Romans that she'd read a few days ago came to mind. It talked about how nothing could separate her from God's love. She located the verse, savoring the words at the end of chapter eight.

The service moved into a time of prayer. She closed her eyes, thankful that Doris had cared enough to guide her in the right direction. Doris had helped her understand how her mother's attitude and behavior had hindered her faith journey.

Before long, the service ended and she stood next to Jack. The center aisle was congested as the congregation moved toward the door.

He smiled. "What did you think?"

"I liked the sermon and the rest was okay."

"What didn't you like?"

"I'm not a big fan of singing and there were five songs."

He raised an eyebrow. "You counted?"

"I didn't know any of the songs."

"I knew a couple but I don't sing."

"Why?"

"I won't scare you off by giving you a demonstration but I'm tone deaf and I don't sing."

"Ever?"

He nodded.

"But aren't you supposed to sing in church? Isn't that an important part of the service?"

His eyes softened. "You really are hung up on the so-called rules. You don't have to sing if you don't want to. God loves you irrespective of whether or not you sing in church."

She reached for her coat and purse, pondering his words.

One of the ladies from the cake stall moved into the row in front of her, a smile beaming on her powdered face. "Kate, it's good to see you. Are you both staying for morning tea?"

She turned to Jack. "Yes, why not?"

Kate held a delicate porcelain teacup balanced on a saucer. After greeting the pastor at the door on her way out, the church ladies had whisked her away from Jack and introduced her to their friends in the church hall. A large table, covered by an array of cakes and sweet treats, was positioned in the middle of the crowded room. Jack stood on the opposite side, talking with a couple of guys she recognized from touch football.

She sipped her last mouthful of tea, meeting his gaze across the room.

He winked, a hint of a smile hovering over his mouth.

She lowered her lashes, heat rising up her neck as she placed her teacup on a nearby table. She straightened the collar of her coat, thankful it was draped over her arm. How could one look from him send all her senses into overdrive?

A petite lady with tight gray curls claimed her attention. "Did you know we have an evening service for the young ones?"

She nodded. "I'm only visiting, and I'll be going home in a few weeks."

"Where do you live, dear?"

"Sydney."

"Oh my, you must find life on a farm very quiet."

She shrugged. "It's a nice change."

"I'm sure Doris enjoys the company. Please send her my regards."

She nodded, trying to remember the lady's name. Mavis. Yes, and Betty was the kind lady standing opposite her.

Jack appeared beside her. "Morning, ladies. I hate to interrupt but we need to get going."

"Sure." She turned to the ladies. "It was good to meet you all."

"Yes, dear," Mavis said, her curls bouncing as she nodded her head. "We hope you'll come again before you leave town."

She smiled, appreciating the time they'd taken to make her feel welcome. "I'll see if I have time to come back."

Jack lifted a brow, his gaze questioning. "Okay, have a good week."

"You, too, and please tell Doris I'll call her later today to check if her asthma is improving," Betty said.

"I will," he said.

Kate waved goodbye and turned to follow Jack.

He wove around the groups of people chatting in the hall before pausing outside the entrance.

She stepped into the bright sunshine, slipping on her coat and squinting to locate her sunglasses in her purse.

He shoved his arms into his jacket. "Are you leaving Snowgum Creek soon?"

"Um, well, I'll be leaving when your parents return and my job is finished." She buttoned up her coat.

"Oh, I thought you'd changed your mind and were leaving early."

She smiled. "You can't get rid of me that easily. I quite like my current job."

His eyes twinkled. "That's good to hear."

She walked with him in silence, stopping when she reached the passenger side of the SUV.

He leaned back against the car. "What do you feel like for lunch?"

"I don't know. Something Doris will like, I guess. I hope she's feeling better."

"The meds should have kicked in by now." He opened her car door.

She settled in her seat, the warm interior a welcome relief from the cold.

He leaped into the driver's seat and switched on the engine.

"I was surprised by how friendly the people were at morning tea."

He grinned. "Doris's friends probably introduced you to half the congregation."

"You mean Betty and Mavis?"

"Yep, and they know everyone."

"So I discovered."

He reversed out of the parking space. "Do you want to go again next week?"

"I think so. At first I was a bit unsure, but after morning tea I feel a lot more comfortable."

"You've experienced country hospitality. They tend to go a bit overboard with the food." He drove along the main street toward the bakery.

"It was an impressive spread and the people I met seemed nice." She twirled a lock of hair around her finger. "They seemed interested in me as a person, rather than wanting to know what I do or who I'm related to."

He drummed his fingers on the steering wheel and pulled into a vacant parking space near the bakery. "Don't take this the wrong way, but I don't think I'd like your church in Sydney."

She stifled a giggle. Jack's nonconformist approach to church wouldn't be appreciated by her mother's circle of friends. "I don't plan on going back to that church." She could do without enduring her mother's social-climbing tactics.

She strolled into the bakery with Jack, inhaling the delectable aroma of freshly baked bread mingled with ground coffee. "Mmm, I'm hungry now."

"Me, too."

They joined the queue in front of the pastry display case. She diverted her gaze, not wanting to be tempted by the treats behind the glass.

"Bread rolls and Doris's favorite tea cake?"

"Good idea."

"And a cappuccino?"

"Yes, please."

"Where do you want to go this afternoon?"

She tilted her head to the side. "Maybe up in the mountains, since there's not much snow at the moment."

"We could drive to Cabramurra. There's often a bit of snow there all year round."

"Really? Even in summer?"

He nodded, moving forward in the line. "It's a couple of hours away, not far from the Snowy Mountains Highway. There's a general store with a café."

"Sounds good. We can have an early lunch before we leave."

"If the weather was warmer, we could visit Yarrangobilly Caves."

"True. I'd like to see the caves one day, and also visit Megan."

"Good idea." He placed their order with the sales assistant.

She collected the cappuccinos while Jack paid the bill. The sweet brew warmed her stomach.

He stashed his wallet in his pocket and she passed over his coffee.

"Thanks." He sipped his cappuccino as they left the bakery. "Why don't we call Megan and line up a visit?"

She lifted a brow. "Do you have time to go to the ski fields?"

"We could leave early and do a day trip. And you have your ski gear at the farm."

She held the bakery items while Jack unlocked the SUV. "I'd love to see Megan, if you're happy to drive?"

"Great. We can call her tonight. I have a couple of Saturdays free and hopefully she can take some time off while we visit."

"Thanks, Jack. I appreciate your showing me around."

"My pleasure." His smile widened. "It's no trouble at all."

Her pulse raced. It looked like she'd lined up a date with Jack. She couldn't wait to see Megan again and spend more time with him.

Chapter 12

Kate leaned back in the passenger seat of Jack's SUV, entranced by the white landscape surrounding her. The snow gum trees lining the edges of the Snowy Mountains Highway were blanketed in pristine white snow.

Jack focused his attention on negotiating the SUV along the winding mountain road. A snow plough had cleared most of the snow off the highway and the early-morning sun had melted some of the ice, creating puddles of water on the road.

Thankfully, Jack had volunteered to do all the driving today. She shivered at the thought of driving on icy roads, even knowing the SUV tires were designed for these conditions. Jack also had snow chains ready to go in the back of the vehicle. She appreciated the lower speed as they traveled around the bends in the road.

Megan awaited their arrival at the ski slopes and she looked forward to seeing her dear friend again. She missed

Megan and was grateful to have a few hours to spend with her. Jack had packed all their skis and snow gear in the SUV.

Kate had last skied a few years ago. She usually tackled the beginner slopes and preferred to play around in the snow.

Memories of her aborted honeymoon filled her mind. It had been Rodney's idea to go skiing in Europe. He loved skiing and, as usual, she'd caved and he'd booked his ideal honeymoon destination. He had everything the way he wanted, with the exception of his uncooperative bride.

Jack tapped his fingers on the steering wheel. "Not far to go now."

"That's fine. I'm happy sitting here and enjoying the view."

"It's something special, isn't it?"

She nodded. "Thanks for driving me to visit Megan."

"No problem. I hardly ever see my little sister these days."

The drive had been pleasant and Jack was a fun driving companion. The easy banter flying between them passed the time quickly. Before long the ski resort town where Megan worked came into view.

Jack parked the SUV and Megan raced over to greet them.

"Kate, it's so good to see you," Megan said as she gave her a big hug.

"Same here."

Megan's exuberance was contagious and Kate smiled. Today was going to be a good day.

"Hey, big bro," Megan said, hugging her brother close.

Kate sighed as she zipped up her ski jacket. It was nice to see two siblings who adored each other. At times like this she wished she wasn't an only child.

Jack ruffled his sister's hair. "You're looking well and happy."

"I'm having a great time. The bumper snowfalls we've had this season have been good for business," Megan said.

"It's good to hear there's lots of work for ski instructors," Kate said. Each winter Megan worked hard at the ski slopes to save for an overseas trip in the springtime.

Megan frowned. "Speaking of which, I feel bad since you've driven all this way but I have lessons I have to teach straight after lunch. I'm sorry. I was hoping to palm them off on another instructor and take the whole day off."

"That's okay." He sent Kate a big smile. "We can amuse ourselves."

"Excellent." Megan hooked her arm through Kate's and whispered in her ear. "Is there something you're not telling me?"

She walked next to Megan to the chairlifts. "What do you mean? I'm finally starting to get back on my feet financially and I'm enjoying my work at the farm."

"I mean you and Jack. We must talk before you go."

"Okay." Kate turned to find Jack following them, lugging all their gear.

Jack grinned, catching up. "So, Meg, how do you want to work this?"

"You can go ahead to the higher slopes and I'll hang down here with Kate."

Kate nibbled her lower lip. "Are you sure? I don't want you to miss out because of me."

"I've organized half-day passes for all of us. If I remember correctly, after about an hour you'll be dying to stash your gear in the SUV and head back to the resort café. I'll meet up with Jack while you sip coffee."

He lifted an eyebrow. "Meg, I'm happy to stay with Kate—"

"You'll have her for the rest of the day. In fact, you see her all the time so it's my turn."

He raised his hands in surrender. "You girls have fun. I'll see you at lunch."

Megan smiled. "I booked a table in the restaurant."

Jack handed Kate the keys to his SUV, his fingertips brushing her knuckles. "I'll see you both soon."

She nodded, an awareness tingling through her hand.

After a final glance and wave, he strode toward the queue for the ski lift.

Kate turned to Megan. "You didn't have to make such a fuss. I could have pottered around down here."

"And miss out on getting a free ski lesson from me?"

"I could muddle along on my own."

She grinned. "The truth is I wanted a chance to talk to you, alone. What's the deal with you and my brother?"

Kate nibbled her lower lip. Of course Megan would pick up on the vibes floating between her and Jack. "We're friends and he's my boss."

"Very close friends, from what I can see." Her eyes sparkled. "Is today's trip here a date?"

She sighed. "I told you, we're friends."

"I find that hard to believe, having witnessed the warm looks shooting between you two." Her smile widened. "I can't believe you've fallen for Jack. It's wonderful. I think you two make a great couple—"

"Whoa, Megan, you're jumping to all the wrong conclusions. In a month or so I'll be going home to Sydney."

"But you don't deny you have feelings for him?"

Kate groaned. "It's complicated. I'll be leaving soon. And don't forget Amy was back in town for the wedding."

"Amy hurt Jack really bad. I don't know what exactly went wrong, but for a while my parents despaired that he'd never get over it. That's why I'm so excited now.

You're the first girl that I know of who he's been seriously interested in and that means a lot."

"But my life is in Sydney and Jack's life is the farm. I can't see the point in starting something, knowing it has to end so soon."

Megan sat on a bench and attached her skis to her boots in one swift motion. "Have you considered the option of living in the country? I've never seen you this relaxed and happy before."

"I don't know." She shrugged. "I guess not living near my mother has made my life less stressful."

"Give things with Jack a chance. See what happens."

"I don't want to hurt anyone." Or get hurt again. After all the problems she'd experienced with Rodney...

"But never exploring what might be, living with a big what-if. Couldn't that be more hurtful at the end of the day?"

"I'm still not sure it's a good idea...."

"Trust me. My brother is one of the good ones. Put aside your fears and just let things evolve. Sometimes you think too much for your own good."

Kate continued to struggle putting on her skis. Maybe Megan was right. Too often she agonized over decisions and ended up doing nothing or acting too late. Her feelings for Jack had taken her by surprise. Over the past few weeks a strong friendship had developed between them. Jack worked all the time but chose to spend most of his free time with her. They shared many common interests and she missed Jack when he wasn't around.

She glanced up at the fluffy white clouds floating around the crisp blue sky. Was it possible to make a decision to be open to new possibilities, whatever they might bring?

She followed Megan to the beginner slopes, pleased that she remembered the basics.

"Okay, Kate, show me what you can do," Megan said.

She successfully negotiated the beginners' run, and a feeling of exhilaration coursed through her.

Megan followed behind soon after.

"Yes, I did it!" she said.

"Way to go, girlfriend. Let's head up to the intermediate runs," Megan said.

Kate grinned. This morning was working out far better than she had anticipated.

Kate heard Megan's voice from across the restaurant. She tucked her novel into her purse and met Jack's gaze. His smile lit up his face and he cut a dashing figure in his ski gear, all lean, hard muscle.

She smiled and he sat opposite, reaching for a menu. "I hear you did well this morning."

Her face warmed as she held his gaze. "I'm officially no longer a beginner. Megan is an excellent teacher."

Megan slid into the seat next to her. "Honestly, Kate, I think you could be a really good skier if you had the opportunity to practice more often."

"How did you two go?" she asked.

He laughed. "We had lots of fun, as usual."

"You nearly came to grief on that bend," Megan said.

"But I didn't, and I returned for lunch unscathed."

Kate grinned. "That's good to hear." A waiter appeared to take their order.

Lunch passed quickly, with Kate enjoying a hearty meat and vegetable pie with a side order of fries and salad. All that energy she had expended skiing had given her an enormous appetite.

Megan sipped the remainder of her latte and glanced at

her watch. "I hate to say it but I must get going. My students are probably already downstairs waiting for me."

Kate rose from her seat and hugged Megan close. "Thanks for everything."

"My pleasure," Megan said.

Megan embraced her brother. "You two enjoy the rest of the day."

"We will," they said in unison.

Megan laughed. "I'm going before I say something that will get me into trouble." She spun around and left the restaurant.

Jack broke the silence between them. "I was thinking we could head up to a tourist lookout not far from here. It's a clear day outside so it should be worthwhile."

"Sounds good."

While Jack finalized their lunch bill, she wandered over to the huge panoramic windows overlooking the slopes. The chairlifts continuously circled up and down the slopes and crowds of skiers negotiated the runs.

Jack stood close behind her and placed his hand on her shoulder. "I'm glad we were out there earlier and missed the big rush."

A tingle of awareness shot through her and the scent of his aftershave tantalized her senses. All she could think about was how right it felt to be near him.

"Kate, are you ready to go?"

She nodded and fell into step beside him.

He caught hold of her hand. She entwined her fingers with his and sighed. What exactly had Megan said to Jack this morning? She hoped it wasn't anything too embarrassing.

She held on to his hand all the way out to the SUV, liking the new direction their relationship was moving.

Jack opened the passenger door to the SUV. He always opened doors for her but now it took on a whole new meaning.

"Thank you."

"My pleasure," he said before walking around to the driver's side.

Half an hour later, the SUV pulled off the main road into a small gravel car park. Jack opened her door and helped her to the ground. He kept hold of her hand as they walked together to a small covered shed that contained the viewing platform.

Kate gasped at the beauty of the white valleys before them. She pulled her phone out of her purse and took half a dozen photos.

He stood close beside her and pointed out the names of the valleys and peaks. The ski village seemed tiny in the distance.

A few minutes later she packed away her phone. "Thank you for suggesting we check out this place. The view is amazing."

He grinned. "I thought you'd like it."

She glanced around, realizing they were alone. "I guess we should head back to the SUV."

Jack reached out and cupped her cheek in his hand. "But first, there's something I've wanted to do all day."

He lowered his head and she closed her eyes, his lips meeting hers. The featherlight kiss tantalized her senses. Warmth filled her heart and she didn't want the moment to end.

He drew back and her brain went to mush. She lowered her gaze for a moment, staring at their entwined hands. What was going on? How could one kiss rock her world off kilter?

He raked his hand back through his windswept hair.

His eyes gleamed with pleasure and his smile broadened. "You never fail to exceed my expectations."

She held his warm gaze and grinned. "Then try this." She reached up and ran her fingers through his wavy hair. She stood on tiptoes and placed her lips on his. Time suspended as she became lost in a world where only they existed.

He took a step back and sucked in a few deep breaths. "We should get going now."

"Do we have to?" A part of her wanted to stay here with him all day.

He nodded. "Otherwise, we may end up in a place that I don't think either of us wants to be in right now."

"You're right." She reined in her galloping thoughts and held his gaze. The connection between them intensified. Talking was a better option.

He draped his arm over her shoulder and walked beside her to the SUV.

Chapter 13

Jack hummed along to the background music playing in the SUV, his mind distracted by the lovely woman sitting beside him. He kept his eyes focused on the winding bends in the highway, hoping for a straight stretch of road in order to sneak a glance in Kate's direction.

She straightened her back and wriggled in the passenger seat, stretching out her legs.

"Are you okay?"

"I think so. My muscles are protesting."

He raised an eyebrow. "But you only skied for an hour."

"I hate to think how I'd feel after a full day on the slopes."

"We'll be home soon." He couldn't forget the feel and taste of her lips, and his desire for a repeat performance. Her presence was intoxicating, distracting, and he needed time to pull back and think with a clear head. Was it wise to pursue something with a woman who had commitment issues and was leaving for good in a matter of weeks?

"Jack, we need to talk."

"Okay, you're sounding very serious. Is something wrong?"

She shook her head. "What just happened back at the lookout?"

"I thought that was obvious."

"I mean between us. We were friends, but now…"

"We're still friends, I hope."

"Well, yes, of course." She paused, as if struggling to find the right words. "I guess I'd like to know where we stand, since you're my boss."

He caught a glimpse of the pensive look in her eyes. "You're very cute when you're flustered."

She threw her hands in the air. "Look, just forget I said anything—"

"No, you're right. We probably should have this conversation."

"I don't want things to become awkward between us."

"As you've probably worked out, I like you a lot and I get the impression you feel the same way."

She nodded. "So where does that leave us?"

"I'd like to get to know you better."

She turned toward him. "Do you mean start dating?"

He nodded. "If that's what you want?"

"But you know I'm leaving soon." She raised her hands, studying her fingernails. "I'm moving back to Sydney when my car is fixed and your parents return."

"They'll be back in a few weeks. We don't need to make any decisions now and we can see how things evolve. But the farm is my life and I can't move away from Snowgum Creek."

"I understand." She nibbled her lower lip, looking like she might say more. "I'll think about it."

"Okay." He swallowed hard, unsure about where his feelings for Kate were headed. One thing he did know was falling for her was a bad idea. She had a history of running away from commitment and he'd already been burned once before. He couldn't expect a sophisticated city girl like Kate to settle for a simple life in the country. Maybe it was for the best that this particular conversation remained unresolved.

Kate tied up the laces on her sneakers, ready to head outside for a run before breakfast. Clouds covered the sun although the ground looked dry. She let herself out the back door, the chilly air bringing goose bumps to her bare arms and legs. Today she planned to run the perimeter fences of the orchards, hoping to catch sight of an emu Jack had spotted hanging around the dam.

She started with a slow jog, warming her stiff muscles before speeding up. The first stretch was downhill, the middle flat and the homestretch uphill.

The orchards were quiet, apart from a couple of pink galahs flying overhead. Jack had risen early and she hoped to see him during her run.

She sipped water from her drink bottle, pacing herself and starting to build up a sweat. She kept an eye on her heart rate monitor watch, checking she wasn't slacking off. This morning she'd be busy reconciling the monthly accounts, and after lunch Jack had enlisted her help in cleaning his vintage car fleet.

She turned the corner, the ground evening off as she ran along the dirt track. Her breathing ragged, she decided to stop at the dam to stretch and have a short recovery.

Ten minutes later she approached the dam. An emu stood

on the other side, his head bobbing as he skirted around the edge of the water. Slowing her pace, she walked over to the dam, capturing the emu's attention. He stood still and stared at her, appearing to be interested in her arrival.

Panting, she sucked in a couple of deep breaths before beginning her stretching routine. Her warm muscles welcomed the break as she released tension in her back and neck, rolling her shoulders.

The sun peeked through the cloud cover, casting a golden glow on the water. A couple of kangaroos hopped through the paddock next door, bounding over a wire mesh fence. *Lord, thank You for providing this oasis of time to reflect and appreciate the beauty of Your creation.*

Her mind dwelled on her difficult relationship with her mother. She was thankful God had forgiven her, but her mother's heart remained hardened. *How can I restore my relationship with my mother if she insists on holding a grudge?*

She wiped her hand over her face, perspiration mixing with salty tears. Maybe Rodney would help her mother see reason. She hadn't heard from him, assuming he'd accepted their breakup and moved on. Her engagement ring was stored in a safe place in her room and she'd have to find a way to return it to him.

She placed her hands on her hips, her breathing back to normal. It was time to conquer the hill back to the house.

Jack's motorbike revved in the distance, the noisy engine growing louder. He pulled the bike to a stop near her, his hair flying in all directions as he planted his feet on the ground.

He grinned. "I see you've found my friend."

Her gaze skittered back to the emu. "He seems happy puttering around the dam."

"Has he chased you yet?"

Her eyebrows shot up. "He wouldn't, would he? I haven't ventured near him on the other side of the dam."

"Emus can be quite social, and sometimes like mingling with people. This one has come near me while I've been working in the orchards."

"How close?"

"Three or four feet away." He ran his hand through his hair, pushing it back off his face. "But if they decide to become affectionate, their beaks can hurt if they peck you."

She shivered. "I guess I'd better start walking slowly up the hill."

"I can stash your drink in the holder and give you a lift back to the house."

"I'm all sweaty and revolting."

He laughed. "And you think I'm not? I can cope with your sweat if you can cope with mine."

The bike looked tempting, and a better proposition than being pecked by a friendly emu. She could finish her run in the orchard near the house.

She passed over her drink bottle. "Don't say I didn't warn you."

His eyes sparkled. "Hop on."

She swung her leg over the bike and wrapped her arms around his waist. His torso was rock hard, all lean muscle under his polar-fleece sweater. She resisted the urge to explore the muscular contours of his back and shoulders.

He revved the engine and they took off up the hill. Her ponytail flew back behind her and the wind whipped her face, invigorating her body. She leaned into his back, cruising at top speed through the orchards. If only this time in her life didn't have to end.

Kate twirled a pencil between her fingers, studying the detailed cooking instructions Doris had given her. How difficult could it be to cook roast lamb with vegetables for dinner tonight?

Dinner had been Jack's idea. Doris had reminded her at breakfast this morning that she'd be having dinner at a friend's house tonight. Jack had cheekily announced that he'd like a roast for dinner, knowing she wasn't the world's best cook.

Later in the morning, he'd presented her with a small leg of lamb to defrost and an array of vegetables from the garden. He had offered to cook, but her feminine pride had insisted she could do it. Being a resourceful girl, she had turned to Doris for help and inspiration.

Doris strolled into the kitchen. "Are you all organized?"

She nodded. "Thanks so much for helping me."

"My pleasure. The lamb has been marinating long enough and needs to go in the oven. I can also help you prepare the vegetables."

"Thanks and I owe you big time for this."

Doris smiled. "It's wonderful seeing my nephew happy and it's all because of you."

Kate raised an eyebrow. "Has Jack said something?"

"No, but I can tell something happened between the two of you last weekend. Plus Jack's allowing you to cook when he's quite capable of making a beautiful roast himself."

"Oh, now I feel even more nervous. I did tell him I'm not a very good cook."

Doris laughed. "Roast lamb is one of his favorites. You'll be fine as long as you get the timing right."

"I hope so." Kate worked alongside Doris, peeling and cutting vegetables, sorting out which ones she'd roast from those she'd steam. Instant gravy mix and bottled mint sauce were the only condiments she needed. Doris had suggested she could make the gravy using the meat juices but Kate had decided too much could go wrong if the gravy didn't thicken properly or she burned it on the stove. A dessert of fruit salad with ice cream had been easy to prepare, with little margin for error.

Doris untied her apron. "You're all set so I'll be on my way. Don't forget to keep an eye on the time."

"Thanks again. Enjoy your evening out."

"I will. I'll be back before ten." Doris shuffled out of the kitchen.

She sighed. The oven timer was set to go off when she next needed to do something. With a little bit of luck, dinner would be ready in an hour. She glanced down at her jeans and T-shirt. She needed to change into something more appropriate. A dark-colored top in case she spilled something would probably be a smart idea.

Kate and Jack had snuck a few moments together, often in the orchards. It was strange, dating someone who was also your boss and lived in the same house. Jack worked hard each day and she didn't see a lot of him, although she had started to think about him all the time.

Tonight was kind of like their first official date and she didn't want to mess it up by ruining dinner. She showered and changed into a navy top and a matching floral skirt. After applying her makeup, she checked her appearance in the full-length mirror in her room. Dressy but understated; she could live with that.

At the sound of the oven timer ringing, she raced back to the kitchen. It was time to turn over the baked vegetables and start steaming the rest of them. She heard the back door close and footsteps in the hallway.

"Kate, I'll shower and be ready for dinner soon," Jack said.

"No problem. I have everything under control."

Before long Kate removed the roast lamb from the oven. She grinned. It was crispy in all the right places.

Jack usually carved the meat for Doris and she'd leave that job for him tonight. According to Doris's instructions, the vegetables in the oven were ten minutes away from being done. She checked on them, relieved they looked good.

Jack entered the kitchen, smiling. "Dinner smells divine and you look cute in that apron."

Kate returned his hug and looked into his eyes. "I've tried really hard to pull everything together."

He dropped a kiss on her lips before stepping back. "I appreciate all your work. I'm also starving and I'll pour you a drink before making a start on carving the lamb."

"Thanks." She sipped her sparkling apple juice and remembered she needed to make gravy when the steamed vegetables were ready. At least that would be easy to do. She followed Jack into the dining room and gasped. The lights were dimmed and two candles were lit in the center of the table. A small gift-wrapped box sat on the corner of the table between the two place settings.

"What do you think?" he asked.

"I love it." She placed her glass on the table and stepped toward him.

"I thought you would," he whispered, stroking her hair.

She tipped her head up and he claimed her lips. Her mind spun in circles and she wished she could do this all day, surrounded by his strong arms, inhaling his masculine scent. Except her brain didn't work too well at times like this and there was something she needed to do.

A burning smell permeated the air, smoke wafted into the dining room and the shrill sound of the smoke alarm filled the house.

She pulled back, widening her eyes. "My vegetables are burning." Had she set the kitchen on fire?

Chapter 14

Jack grabbed Kate's hand and they raced into the kitchen. Smoke rose from the steamer on the cooktop.

He switched off the stove and filled the bottom of the steamer with water. The acrid scent intensified as steam rose from the saucepan in the sink.

"I'm so sorry." She pressed her lips together, blinking rapidly as if to hold back tears.

"It's okay." He glanced at the blackened base of the saucepan. "The saucepan will be as good as new after we soak it overnight."

"But my greens are ruined." She stood beside him, staring at the overcooked and soggy vegetables in the steamer. "We can't eat this."

He lightly held her shoulders, a smile tugging at the corner of his mouth. "It's okay. The lamb is perfect and I'll check on the veggies in the oven."

He opened the oven door and inhaled the divine aroma

of roast lamb and vegetables. He lifted out the tray and smiled. "These look good."

"But the pumpkin pieces are black around the edges." She shook her head. "I'm sorry. I followed Doris's instructions and I don't know what I did wrong—"

"It's fine." He placed the oven glove on the kitchen counter and held her face in his hands. "I like my pumpkin overdone. It's all good."

She lifted her gaze and stared into his eyes. "Are you sure?"

He nodded. "I'll put the kettle on to boil water for the gravy and we can serve up in here."

"I still feel bad that I ruined the greens."

"Trust me, not having peas and broccoli won't kill us. And you're not the only one who has boiled a steamer dry." He started carving up the succulent lamb, cooked to perfection.

"You've done this before?"

He cringed. "More than once. Doris can tell you a few stories later."

She placed two dinner plates on the counter and served up the roast vegetables.

He added a generous serving of sliced lamb to their plates, his taste buds ready to appreciate the tender meat.

The electric kettle switched itself off and she scooped the gravy mix into a measuring cup, adding water to form a thick mixture.

He carried their plates into the dining room and she followed close behind with the condiments. He pulled out a chair and she slipped into her seat, a smile tilting up her lips.

Kate sampled her first mouthful of lamb, her eyes sparkling. "The lamb is good."

He grinned. "Everything is good. You've done well, all things considered."

"I can't take all the credit. Doris was very helpful."

"I'll remember to thank her later." He reached over and handed her the gift-wrapped box.

"Jack, you didn't need to give me a gift...."

"I wanted to. It's something I saw the other day in Sunny Ridge and I thought of you."

She removed the wrapping paper and opened the lid of the box. Two brilliant sapphire stud earrings lay inside the box.

Her smile widened. "I love them. Jack, I don't know what to say. Thank you."

He held her hand across the table. "I'm glad you like them."

"I do." She lifted the earrings out of the box, taking a closer look. "They match my sapphire pendant."

"I'd like to take you out next Saturday night. How about we have dinner and catch a movie in Sunny Ridge?"

She nodded. "Sounds good. I've missed going to the movies."

"And if the weather is clear tomorrow afternoon we could go for a drive somewhere."

"I'd like that."

Before long she rose from the table and started clearing their plates. "What game are we playing tonight? Or do you want to watch a movie?"

"I'm in the mood for Monopoly but if you want to play Scrabble instead, we can do that."

"Then Monopoly it is. Do you want to start before or after dessert?"

He stood up, walked over to her and encircled his arms around her waist. "Before dessert, but there's something else I want to do now."

He lowered his head and his mouth met hers. She welcomed his kiss and all the familiar sensations raced through him.

Moments later she drew back and gazed into his eyes. "Thank you, Jack, for everything. The earrings are beautiful."

His heart swelled. "I'm looking forward to seeing you wear them."

"Next weekend," she promised.

Kate finished entering the last invoice and closed the accounting software program. It was past time for her afternoon coffee break. She glanced out the window at the gray sky. The ground was still icy in places from the low temperature and dense overnight frost.

Jack had left early this morning to buy farm supplies from Sunny Ridge and he wasn't due back until later this afternoon.

Kate walked up the hallway to the kitchen. Doris sat huddled at the kitchen table, breathing in air through a face mask attached to a ventilator.

She rushed to her side. "Are you okay?"

She nodded and spoke slowly in small spurts. "This is helping. I need to see my doctor."

"When did the asthma start?"

"Not long ago. My chest felt a little tight when I woke this morning."

Kate reached for the phone. "Is your doctor's phone number in the address book?"

Doris nodded. "Under D. Dr. Davidson."

Kate located the number and spoke to the receptionist. Dr. Davidson could meet Doris at the hospital that afternoon.

Kate wrote down the directions. She agreed to leave

with Doris immediately, a faster option than waiting for an ambulance to come out from Snowgum Creek.

"Okay, Doris, we're driving into town now to see Dr. Davidson at the hospital."

"Thanks. This thing runs on batteries and I can use it in the car."

Kate left a message for Jack on his phone before leaving. The weather looked ominous and she made the decision to drive the SUV, glad Jack had taken the truck this morning.

She helped settle Doris in the SUV and sucked in a deep breath. Her heart raced. She hadn't driven on the road since before the accident.

Lord, please give me the strength to survive this drive and deliver Doris safely to the hospital.

She reversed out of the garage. A few rays of sunlight broke through the clouds and the icy grass beside the drive shone like crystals.

Kate bit her lip. She could get through the fifteen-minute drive into town. Doris's breathing sounded steadier. She cautiously negotiated the drive and turned onto the road.

The winding road required her full attention. She passed the tree her car had slid into and shivered. Bad memories resurfaced and fear continued to gnaw at her stomach.

Thankfully, they only passed a couple of cars traveling the other way during the trip. Kate let out a big breath when the town came into view.

She parked the SUV outside the hospital entrance and waited while they brought out a wheelchair for Doris. A nurse attended to Doris straightaway and Kate took a seat in the waiting room. She flipped through a number of women's magazines, her mind preoccupied by Doris' health crisis.

A woman sat beside her. "Hi, Kate."

Kate turned to find Amy sitting next to her, a welcoming smile on her face.

"Oh, hi," Kate said.

"I didn't mean to startle you."

"No, you're fine. I'm a little distracted. Doris has had a bad asthma attack."

"Is she okay?"

"I think so. I'm waiting on word from her doctor."

"Is Jack here?"

She shook her head. "He's at Sunny Ridge. I left a message on his phone and I assume he's on his way."

A doctor appeared and called out Amy's name.

Amy stood. "Please send my regards to Doris. I'll duck in and see her before I leave."

"No problem."

Amy disappeared into an examination room.

The last person Kate had expected to see this afternoon was Amy. When had she arrived back in town? What would Jack think when he learned Amy was at the hospital?

Doris's doctor appeared in the waiting room and called Kate into the examination room.

Kate entered the sparse room and took a seat beside Doris's bed. Doris sat upright in the bed, and color had returned to her cheeks. The doctor explained that he'd given Doris medication to stabilize her breathing and she needed to rest for the next few days.

The doctor left and she rearranged the pillows behind Doris's back. "I'm glad to see you're looking better."

"The doctor thinks the cold snap has set off my asthma."

"Did the doctor say how long you'll be staying in hospital?"

"I'm not sure." She raised her left arm. "I'm attached to this drip for the time being."

"By the way, Amy said to send you her regards."

"Amy." Doris frowned. "She must be back to help her mother. Did she say why she was at the hospital?"

She shook her head. "I've no idea but she did say she might call in later to visit you."

"That would be nice. I only had a brief chat with her at the wedding and the poor girl was having a difficult night." She held the oxygen mask, sucking in deep breaths. "I hope she's okay."

A light knock sounded on the door. Amy stood on the threshold, a hesitant expression shadowing her pretty face.

"Come in, dear." Doris pulled herself up higher in the bed. "How is your mother doing?"

Unshed tears glistened in Amy's eyes. "She's putting on a brave face but I know the chemo is taking a lot out of her." She turned to Kate. "My mother is fighting breast cancer and thankfully has a good prognosis."

"I'm sorry," Kate said. "I hope the chemo goes okay."

"Me, too." Amy dropped into a seat on the other side of the bed. "And how are you doing? It looks like you've given Kate quite a scare today."

"I'll be fine." Doris reached for Amy's hand. "How are you coping with everything?"

Amy lowered her lashes. "I'm on holidays from university and came home to help Mom and Dad."

"What about your husband? Is he with you?"

She shook her head. "He's busy with work. And I needed to get away." Her lower lip quivered. "Last week I miscarried again."

Doris tightened her grip on Amy's hand. "Oh, dear, I'm so sorry."

Kate met Amy's watery gaze. "Are you okay? Is there anything we can do?"

"Not really. I was fourteen weeks along this time, the

longest I've gone before something went wrong." Her shoulders slumped. "We're going to try IVF next."

"I hope everything works out for you. I'm an only child because my mother had difficulties falling pregnant and had a number of miscarriages. Hang in there. Modern technology can do a lot these days."

"I know. It has been a long road. My husband is quite a bit older than me and desperate to have a child soon."

Doris looked Amy straight in the eye. "Don't you go beating yourself up and blaming yourself for these problems. If it's meant to be it will happen. My dear husband and I wanted children and it didn't happen, but we didn't let it ruin our lives. I adore my nieces and nephews and life is too short to live with regrets."

"I guess you're right." Amy blinked and dabbed at the corners of her eyes with her index fingers.

Footsteps sounded outside the room. Kate looked up to find Jack in the doorway. "Amy? What are you doing here?"

Chapter 15

Jack strode into the room, startled to see Amy at Doris's bedside. "Is everything fine?"

Amy nodded. "I just stopped by to check on Doris. Mom is having her chemo treatment today." She glanced at her watch. "Actually, I'd better get going in a few minutes."

"Okay." He turned to his aunt. "How are you doing?"

"It was just a bad asthma attack and I'm glad Kate was nearby to help me."

"I worry about you when you're on your own." His aunt sounded breathless and looked frail, her arm hooked up to a drip. What would have happened if Kate hadn't been at the farm? *Lord, thank You for looking after Doris today.*

Doris smiled. "You worry about everyone."

"It's my job." He was responsible for the farm while his parents were away.

Kate wriggled in her seat and stretched her arms back

above her head. "Thanks for coming straight here. I hope my message didn't send you into a panic."

He raised an eyebrow. "I knew you'd look after Doris."

"Yes, she took good care of me," Doris said.

Amy gathered her purse and stood. "I must go. Doris, you take care and I may see you all in town if I stay for a couple more weeks."

Jack nodded. "Pass on my regards to your mother."

"I will," she said before leaving the room.

Jack sat in the chair Amy vacated. "Is Amy okay? She's looking pale and very thin."

Doris met his gaze, her eyes softening. "She has a lot happening in her life and needs her friends." She glanced at Kate and then back at him, her forehead wrinkling. "I'm glad you and Amy are friends again."

He nodded. "All water under the bridge." He'd made his peace with Amy and he was worried about her. She'd lost the vibrancy and larger-than-life personality that he remembered, and had become quiet and withdrawn.

Kate slouched back in her seat, her brows drawn together. He wasn't sure how to interpret her silence.

A nurse came into the room and he moved to the side with Kate while the nurse checked Doris's chart.

She stood up and he inhaled the sweet scent of her perfume. He looked deep into her eyes. "How are you doing? It's been a rough day."

She nodded. "The drive here wasn't as bad as I thought it would be."

He brushed a loose curl back off her face. "You did well and conquered your fear."

"But now I have to drive home in the dark."

The nurse hung up the chart. "I'll finish up the paperwork and Doris can be discharged soon."

Doris's face brightened. "Thank goodness. This drip is driving me mad."

The nurse left the room and returned minutes later with a wheelchair. Doris settled her account with the receptionist and they helped her back to the car.

Jack settled Doris in the passenger seat of the SUV before switching his attention to Kate. "You can follow me home and I promise I'll take it slow."

She nodded, frown lines prominent between her brows.

"Thanks for driving Doris to the hospital." He held her gaze. "I know how hard this has been for you."

"I'll be happier once we're back at the farm."

He lifted her hands, wound together so tight that her knuckles had turned white. He brushed his lips over the back of each hand. "Take a deep breath. The afternoon sun has melted a lot of the ice. We'll be fine."

He separated her hands, holding one in each of his own. "You can do this, Kate. Baby steps, remember."

She nodded. "I'd better get in the SUV before I lose my nerve."

He opened the driver's door. "Drive safe. I'll pray for you."

A hint of a smile tilted up the corner of her lips. "You, too, and thanks. I need all the prayers I can get."

Kate fastened her seat belt and shoved the SUV key into the ignition. Pretty hues of pink and orange covered the western sky. She gripped the steering wheel, memories of the big gray kangaroo lingering in her mind.

Doris placed a comforting hand on her arm. "Are you okay, dear?"

She sucked in a deep breath, attempting to calm her racing pulse. "I'll be fine. I just have to keep driving."

"It'll get easier, and I'd drive home if I could."

"I'm sorry."

"Don't apologize. Your car accident was scary and I understand your fears."

She nodded.

Doris reached for her hand. "Why don't I pray for us now? Ask the Lord to give you courage for the drive home and banish your fears."

"Okay." She closed her eyes, reassured by the thought of her heavenly Father looking after her.

"Lord, please be with Kate as we drive home and give her the strength to overcome her anxiety and fears. Amen."

"Amen." A feeling of peace washed over her and she opened her eyes, ready to face the drive home. "Thanks, Doris."

"You're welcome."

Jack had pulled over ahead of her and she followed him to the parking lot exit.

Doris lounged back in her seat, her sharp gaze focused on the road. "I'll keep an eye out for roos."

"Thanks. That will be a big help."

"I know their usual spots, and I'll give you fair warning on where you need to slow down."

The SUV crawled along the main street, busy with people stopping in at the stores after work. "Maybe we should buy something for dinner in town?"

"No need. I have beef casserole defrosting in the fridge."

She smiled. "Mmm, sounds great." Doris had spoiled her with her fabulous cooking, which she would miss when she left Snowgum Creek in a few weeks' time.

She followed Jack's truck as he turned onto the road heading out to the farm. She flicked on her headlights, the darkness creeping in as the sun sank lower behind the horizon. The winding road was challenging to drive, and she appreciated Jack easing off the gas pedal. She maintained a large gap between the SUV and his truck, just in case he came across a kangaroo.

"You know, Kate, I'm really going to miss you when you return to Sydney."

She swallowed hard, unexpected tears threatening to form in her eyes. "I'll miss you, too." And Jack. She didn't want to think about saying goodbye to him, or contemplate whether they had a future together. He'd become an important part of her life and she dreaded the day when her current job would end.

Her car should be ready to collect soon, after waiting weeks for the necessary parts to be shipped to the garage in Snowgum Creek. She sighed. It was time to start applying for jobs in Sydney.

She drove along the stretch of road where she had the accident, resisting the strong desire to close her eyes. Her chest tightened and she lifted her foot off the accelerator, hoping to calm her coiled nerves. No kangaroos were in sight and she was relieved when they turned onto the track leading up to the orchards.

"I survived." They bounced over the grate at the entrance to the farm. Doris activated the remote for the garage door and she parked the SUV in its usual spot.

Doris unclipped her seat belt. "See, I told you we'd be fine."

"I'm glad it's over." She hoped driving would become easier. If not, she'd be in for a long and arduous trip back home to Sydney.

Kate closed the accounting software package and stretched out her arms and legs. After two hours of entering data, her back demanded she get out of her chair and walk somewhere. She glanced at the time on the computer. Eleven-thirty. Her stomach rumbled. Time for an early lunch.

Her phone rang and she checked the caller ID. Her mother; the second time she'd called this morning. She pressed the talk button too late again and the call transferred to voice mail. A minute later she checked her messages, disappointed to discover her mother hadn't felt the need to leave a message. Or an apology.

After their last conversation, she wasn't keen to talk with her mother if her attitude hadn't changed. She sighed. She couldn't avoid talking to her forever, especially now that she had started applying for jobs in Sydney.

She had woken at six this morning and spent a few hours in the orchards before starting on the paperwork. Jack had been sick with the flu for the past week. He'd given her a list of things to do and check up on in the orchards. The crisp morning air had inspired her to get moving, and she'd worn four layers of clothing as she carried out the outdoor tasks.

Doris had fully recovered from her asthma attack two weeks earlier but she was staying away from Jack as a precaution. Poor Jack had been confined to his room, and Kate had picked up extra tasks around the house and orchards to help out while he was ill.

Kate carried her coffee mug into the kitchen. She found Jack leaning on the kitchen counter, cradling a mug in his hands.

"Hey, how are you feeling?" she asked.

"Much better this morning." He sipped his tea. "I'm hoping I'll be well enough to go back to work in the orchards tomorrow."

She frowned, switching on the kettle. "Didn't the doctor say you needed a few more days of bed rest?"

"I need to check up on things and I have maintenance

work to do on the cars. The aches and pains have finally gone away."

"That's good news. But you don't need to worry about the orchards. I did everything on the list this morning."

He raised an eyebrow. "Really? I thought it would take you longer...."

"I'm more efficient than you think." A grin tugged at the corner of her mouth. "I like working in the orchards and everything is fine."

"Okay." He smiled. "I trust you to do a good job. Now that my nose is starting to look and feel normal again, I'll brave the wind chill tomorrow and see for myself."

She found a clean mug and added a tea bag. "You'd be better off working on the cars in the shed, where you're out of the wind."

"You're probably right."

"I am." She poured boiling water into her mug. "Are you hungry? I'll make a platter of sandwiches for lunch. Doris is visiting friends in town for most of the day."

"Sounds good. I've tried to stay away from Doris so I don't make her sick."

"She's doing fine. I'm glad I was vaccinated a few months back." She had done all the necessary vaccinations in preparation for her overseas honeymoon. A cold chill crawled along her spine. If Rodney hadn't changed his itinerary, he'd be arriving back in Australia any day now.

"Have you had time to work on the accounts?"

She nodded. "As of ten minutes ago, everything is totally up-to-date, and I don't have any more work to do. Sometime before the end of the week you need to make a few internet payments."

"Sure. I'll look at the payments after lunch."

"Also, I've started lining up job interviews in Sydney."

His eyes widened. "When?"

"Maybe next week or the week after. I need to confirm the interview times."

"So soon?"

"My work here is done and Doris said your parents will be back any day now. Actually, I forgot to tell you that your mom is due to call you now."

Minutes later, the phone rang and Jack picked up the handset.

Kate sipped her tea and started preparing their sandwiches. She couldn't help overhearing his conversation with his mother.

"Mom, I'm feeling much better and I'll be right as rain in a few days," he said.

She opened the fridge and selected the sandwich fillings.

His hand lingered on her shoulder and he smiled, pointing to the door.

She nodded, acknowledging his need to talk to his mother in private.

"You're coming home next week?" Jack said as he left the kitchen.

Next week. Her stomach sank. Her idyllic job had come to an end.

Chapter 16

Jack strode down the hall to the study, holding the phone as he listened to his mother talk about Grandpa's health.

He slowed his pace, disappointment weighing down his heart. Even if Kate was prepared to stay, his parents' imminent return would bring her job on the farm to an end. "Does this mean Grandpa and Grandma don't need you anymore?"

"That's right. We're leaving tomorrow and we'll take our time driving home on the Pacific Highway."

"Enjoy the warmer weather while you can."

"We will."

"You have a letter from your Aunt Mary somewhere." He rifled through a pile of correspondence on his desk. "Maybe a card."

"Don't worry about it. I'll catch up on the mail next week. How's the farm going?"

"All the accounts and paperwork are up-to-date, thanks

to Kate. I don't know how I would have survived without her."

"Good news."

"And Kate's finishing up at the end of the week. She's lining up job interviews in Sydney."

"How do you feel about her leaving?"

He frowned. What was his mother up to now? "I'll miss having her around, but the job is done and she's returning to her old life in Sydney."

"You sound very calm." She paused. "I hear you've been spending nearly all your free time with Kate."

"Have you been talking to my sister?"

"A few days ago—"

"Meg needs to learn to mind her own business."

Silence filled the phone line for a few moments. "I just want you to be happy and Kate is a lovely girl."

"Her car will be ready any day, and then she's free to go."

"But I thought you two were dating?"

He tightened his grip on the phone. "Mom, I know you mean well but Kate is a city girl. Her life is in Sydney."

"You sound very matter-of-fact." She paused. "You really like her, don't you?"

"Mom, can we drop it?"

"I know she was a runaway bride, but your sister assures me it was exceptional circumstances that led Kate to make such a rash decision."

He let out a deep breath. "Okay, I do care for Kate but I'm being realistic. I can't expect her to settle for a quiet country life. All her friends and family are in Sydney."

"If you really like her, and I can tell you do, then don't let her slip through your fingers. Love isn't always easy to find."

"Mom, I know what you're saying, but I will handle

this my way." He couldn't ask Kate to give up her big-city dreams. She'd only hate him for it later when she became bored with farm life.

"I worry about you, Jack. You spend too much time working. How will you ever find a wife if you keep working all the time?"

A smile tilted up the corners of his mouth. "I know you want grandchildren. Go bug Megan."

His mom huffed. "As if Megan will settle down anytime soon. She can barely live in one spot for a few months, let alone think about marriage and kids. Who would have her?"

He laughed. "You should have had a third child who could provide grandchildren. Meg and I are both lost causes."

"I don't know." She dropped her voice to a whisper. "I'm not giving up on you yet. At least you're settled in one place."

"True. I guess I'll see you and Dad sometime next week." He left the study and headed back to the kitchen.

"Tell Doris I'll call on our way back into town and stock up the pantry."

"No problem." He ended the call and found Kate reading a book in the living room, her beautiful hair falling over her face.

She looked up and smiled. "I have lunch ready in the kitchen."

"Great. My parents will be home early next week."

"I'm sure you can't wait to see them again."

He nodded. "Mom's very happy that you've put all the admin in order."

"I'm glad I could help." She walked ahead of him to the kitchen.

"Have you made arrangements for next week?"

"I have two interviews scheduled." She sighed. "I'm going to live with my parents until I find a job."

He grunted. "You don't sound too excited."

The phone rang and he answered the call before passing it to Kate. "The local garage."

She nodded and held the handset close to her ear.

"Yes, Friday will be fine. Thanks." She ended the call.

He clenched his jaw. "Your car is ready?"

"Friday lunchtime, if that's okay with you?"

"Sure." He poured a mug of coffee, his hand unsteady. "You know you can stay as long as you need."

"Yes, but I need to get organized. I was thinking I might visit Megan on my way home and drive back the coast road."

"When is your first interview?"

"Thursday. If I leave here Saturday, I can stay with Megan a few days and take my time driving home."

Saturday. He felt like a brick had lodged deep in his heart. She was leaving in three days. But he couldn't ask her to stay. Not when he knew she yearned for her urban lifestyle. "The South Coast is beautiful."

"So I've heard. I'll go online and check out accommodations." She ate her last sandwich and stood. "I should start packing."

Packing. He drew in a deep breath. "Do you need any help?"

She shook her head. "It won't take me long." She glanced at her watch. "Time for me to get back to work. Is it okay if I finish up tomorrow?"

He nodded. "I think I'll take Friday off, too. Maybe we could do something in the afternoon. Go for a drive?"

She smiled. "Sounds good. I'd like to take a few photos before I leave." She spun around and walked out of the room.

He sank into a chair, his head resting in his hands. How

could he let her go? Was his mother right? Was he afraid to risk having his heart broken again because she was a runaway bride?

The midmorning sun streamed through the window of the SUV. Jack sat in the driver's seat beside Kate, seemingly deep in thought. He'd been quiet since she'd announced on Wednesday that she was leaving tomorrow.

They drove into town to collect her car. But first they were going to check the mail, grab a coffee and spend some time walking in the park. Kate wanted to take a few photos.

Jack pulled into a parking space opposite the park. He jumped out and opened her door.

She smiled. "Latte?"

"Definitely."

She ducked into a nearby café and purchased their coffee while Jack visited the post office. She waited for him on a bench outside in the sun, sipping her latte.

Minutes later he strode down the steps, holding a bundle of mail, a large parcel tucked under his arm. "You have half a dozen letters."

"Really? That's unusual." She accepted the mail, flicking through the envelopes that all came from the same company.

"Wait here and I'll stash the parcel in the SUV."

"Okay." She ripped open one of the letters and gasped, reading the content. She shook her head. How could she be so stupid?

The letter of demand from a store credit card debt collector burned her fingers. How could she have forgotten about the dresses and shoes she'd bought to attend a number of society functions with Rodney? New season designer labels that had been way outside her budget.

Uncomfortable memories rose to the surface. Her credit

card had been maxed and she'd signed up for the store account. They had issued the account without hesitation due to her high income from her previous job. Why had she never received the card or any statements?

She tore open the other letters, realizing they had listed the wrong address on her account. Her stomach sank. They'd found her and she owed an enormous amount of money due to the ridiculously high interest rate. Money she didn't have unless she acquired a job next week and started work straightaway.

Her plans to visit Megan and travel home via the South Coast evaporated. She needed that money as a bargaining tool to start a repayment schedule as soon as possible.

She bit her lip, tears forming in her eyes. Jack had been waylaid by an elderly lady across the street. She stashed the letters in her purse and tried to pull herself together. He didn't need to learn that her financial ineptitude had reached a whole new level.

He waved and dashed across the road. "Sorry I took so long. I can't walk through this town without someone wanting to stop and chat."

She nodded and sipped her latte, her mind reeling as she processed the latest disaster in her life. They walked along the main street in silence before heading into the park.

The lush grass glistened under a cloudless sky. Blossom trees were starting to bud and a gentle breeze whistled through the taller gum trees clustered at one end of the park.

He reached for her hand. "Are you okay?"

"I'm fine." She shot him a bright smile, hoping he'd drop the subject. For the past few months she'd lived in his world and had forgotten the harsh realities of her world. She was a failure in so many ways and she couldn't bear for him to learn the truth.

She strolled beside Jack on the paved path, trying to act normal and pausing to take a photo of a rosella perched beside a fountain.

"Kate, I've been wondering about something." His tone sounded serious.

Her heart skipped a beat. "What is it?"

He rubbed his hand through his windswept hair. "You don't have to answer if you don't want to. It's probably none of my business."

She grabbed hold of his hand, energized by the warmth emanating from his fingers entwined with hers. "What's bothering you?"

He stopped, turning to face her. "What went wrong with Rodney? Why did you run?"

She closed her eyes, her lower lip trembling. Did he have to ask this question now, when her life was spiraling out of control?

"I found out one of his secrets."

"Did he cheat on you?"

"Not that I know of, but then I learned he didn't share much of his life with me. I found out by accident that he was selling Rosewood."

"Rosewood. You mean the house in Sydney rented by the charity that helps teen moms?"

She nodded, blinking away the moisture in her eyes. "Sarah lived there after her parents kicked her out."

"Where's Sarah now?"

"Happily married in London with child number two on the way. Her son, James, is now seven and gets on really well with his English stepfather. They would have come out for the wedding except Sarah was having complications with her pregnancy."

"When is she due?"

"Next month. I haven't heard from her in a while and I assume all is well."

He frowned. "Did Rodney know about Sarah?"

"Yes. I did volunteer work at Rosewood, and I actually met Rodney there around the time he was purchasing the property."

"So he should understand the sentimental value it holds."

She nodded, tightening her grip on his hand. "I found the development application in his study a few days before the wedding." She met his gaze, heartened by the concern radiating from his eyes. "I asked him about it and he said he'd always planned to redevelop Rosewood, knock it down and build apartments."

"Did he know you were upset?"

She shook her head, thankful when he passed a tissue to wipe away the rogue tears escaping her eyes. "He was so casual in the way he spoke. He told me not to worry, that he'd help the charity find a new location for their services, as if that made it all better." She sipped her coffee, the warm liquid taking away the chill in her bones from thinking about Rodney.

"But it didn't." He swiped a loose lock of hair back off her face, his fingers lingering on her cheek. "Did you tell him then that you didn't want to marry him?"

"I was in shock, and felt so betrayed. I'd shared my plans to work more hours at Rosewood as a volunteer after our honeymoon, and he never said a word." She pressed her fingers over her eyelids. "He'd known for months that he was redeveloping the site, and said nothing…."

"And that was the ultimate betrayal."

She nodded. "It wasn't the fact he was redeveloping Rosewood that bothered me most. He was dishonest and didn't tell me the truth up front. How could I trust him if he thought it was okay to keep such a big secret from me?"

He draped his arm over her shoulders and gave her a hug. "I get it. And you tried to talk to your mother and she wouldn't listen."

She snuggled into the brief embrace, disappointed when he stepped away and sipped his coffee. "It was horrible. I think the resentment built up inside me and on my wedding day I was angry and knew I had to run."

"It's okay. Rodney is in the past." He held her gaze for a few moments, empathy radiating from his gorgeous eyes.

She lowered her lashes, longing for Jack to be a part of her future and knowing it was an impossible dream. "I hope so. Mom says he still wants to marry me, but I think she's exaggerating. He's probably back in Australia and I really don't want to see him again."

He reached for her hand, his finger caressing her fingertips. "You're safe here."

"I know." She met his warm gaze. "I've really enjoyed my time here with you and Doris and I hope your parents will be happy with my work."

His eyes twinkled. "They're delighted to know they're not coming home to a pile of paperwork. Mom was hoping to thank you in person...."

She started walking back to the car. "I must go back to Sydney tomorrow." She fell into step beside Jack, her fingers entwined with his. Inside, her heart was breaking. She had grown to love this quaint little town, and Jack's farm. She'd miss the peace and tranquility of the open spaces. She inhaled the sweet perfume from the roses lining the pebbled path. And she'd miss Jack. More than she dared to admit.

Chapter 17

Kate tasted a spoonful of chicken and sweet corn soup. The Chinese restaurant in Snowgum Creek was doing a roaring trade, and Jack had been lucky to secure a table on a busy Friday night.

"How's your soup?" He sat across from her, their table in a secluded corner of the restaurant.

"Very nice, thanks."

He dipped a spring roll into a tiny bowl of sweet chili sauce. "What time are you planning to leave tomorrow?"

"After breakfast, maybe around nine. I might stop in the Southern Highlands for a late lunch."

"Good idea." He paused. "Or, you could stay longer in Snowgum Creek."

His unspoken question lingered between them. "Jack, you know I can't."

"Why?" He rubbed his hands over his face, fatigue shadowing his eyes. "I thought you liked living here."

"I do." She concentrated on eating her soup, dodging his question.

He reached for her hand and laced his fingers through hers. "What aren't you telling me?"

She closed her eyes, unable to avoid the moment of truth. He deserved to know that her reasons for leaving had nothing to do with him.

"Please, Kate, help me understand why you must go tomorrow."

She blinked. "It's all my fault. I've messed up again."

"How?"

His gentle question prompted her to share her painful story. "I have to find a job in Sydney."

"You could stay longer at the farm and look for a job in town."

She shook her head. "There aren't any full-time positions in my line of work in Snowgum Creek."

"Have you looked?"

"It's pointless. The salaries aren't competitive with what I could earn in Sydney."

He let go of her hand. "This is all about money?"

She lowered her lashes, avoiding his piercing gaze. "Yes."

He leaned back in his chair and crossed his arms over his chest. "I didn't realize a big-city career was that important to you."

"It's not that simple." She sipped her water, her throat dry. "I have unexpected bills to pay."

He frowned. "I thought you had the car repair costs covered?"

"I do. It's not that. Remember those letters we collected this afternoon?"

He nodded.

She sucked in a deep breath. "They're from a debt collector."

His mouth fell open. "Are you serious?"

"Yep."

"How long have you known about this debt?"

She squirmed in her seat, twirling her spoon between her fingers. "I forgot about a store card."

"You what? Why isn't the card burning a hole in your purse? Did you ignore the monthly account statements?"

"I didn't actually receive the card or the statements because they had the wrong address details on file."

He shook his head. "And you never thought to check? How did you run up debt without having the card?"

"Um, I kind of spent all the money on the day I applied for the card."

"Why did you need this card? Don't you already have a credit card?"

She nodded. "The thing is, my credit card was maxed and I had to buy stuff to wear out to a couple of social events."

He narrowed his eyes. "Are you telling me this debt is from buying clothes and shoes?"

"I couldn't be seen in the same outfit twice. Rodney had very high expectations when it came to my appearance."

A waiter cleared away their plates and set the table for their next course.

"If all this expenditure was for Rodney, why didn't he pay for it?"

Heat rose up her neck and covered her cheeks. "Well, actually, he was going to take care of all my debts after we married."

"That figures." He drummed his fingers on the table. "How much money are we talking about? Hundreds? Thousands?"

She fidgeted with a sapphire earring, his beautiful gift a reminder of why she was unworthy of him. "The second one."

"I assume the interest rate and late penalty fees have escalated the initial debt into some astronomical amount."

"Yep. It's a big disaster and I have a letter of demand I must pay by the end of next week to prevent further legal action."

"Do you have the money to cover the first payment?"

She nodded. "That's why I'm not visiting Megan or driving home via the South Coast. The payment will take most of my savings, and I'll stay with my parents until I can get back on my feet financially."

"I could lend you some money—"

"No, I have to take responsibility for my incompetence. I'm not asking my father to help me out, either. I need to make this situation right by paying my own way."

He nodded, his mouth drawn into a grim line.

"I know I've disappointed you…."

"This isn't exactly the conversation I'd hoped we'd be having tonight."

"Me, either. I wish I could turn back the clock and make different choices, but I have to live with the consequences whether I like it or not."

"How long will it take you to get the debt paid off?"

She held his gaze, pleading for his understanding. "At least three or four months, assuming I live with my parents and stick to a very tight budget. Maybe longer."

He muttered something under his breath and squared his shoulders. "Is your credit card still maxed, as well?"

"No, I cleared the full balance owing this month and only have a few hundred dollars to pay next month."

"Well, at least that's one good thing."

"I'm sorry, Jack. I've learned a hard lesson and I won't make the same mistake again."

The waiter returned with their next course, placing a couple of plates of meat dishes and rice in the center of the table. She cast a cursory glance over the food, her appetite gone.

"What would you like first?" he asked. "Beef or chicken?"

"Chicken, please, but only a small serving."

He spooned fried rice and satay chicken onto her plate before serving a generous helping on his own plate. At least her financial woes hadn't diminished his appetite.

She picked up her chopsticks and sampled the chicken. The spicy flavors blended beautifully and she was determined to eat her portion.

"Kate."

His soft tone of voice snagged her attention and she lifted her gaze. "Yes."

"Is there anything I can do or say to change your mind about leaving tomorrow?"

Her heart splintered into pieces as she held back tears. "No, I wish there was but I have to go."

The next morning Jack put the breakfast bowls and plates in the dishwasher, his heart heavy. He'd already checked the tire pressure on Kate's car and made sure the engine was in good order and the fluid levels topped up. She needed to update her car to a newer model, but that wasn't going to happen until she cleared her debts.

He shook his head, perplexed by everything he had learned last night over dinner. He couldn't fathom how she had gotten herself into such a dire financial situation. His parents had taught him the importance of saving money to buy the things he needed. He always cleared the full balance on his credit card every month, only making purchases that he knew he could afford to cover. He'd built up his fleet of vintage cars by saving to buy each new addition.

The family had borrowed money to install hail netting in the orchards, but that expenditure had paid for itself tenfold over the following years. He couldn't imagine going into debt to buy frivolous items. Or forgetting about a loan altogether.

Doris walked into the kitchen, her face downcast. "Are you able to help Kate carry her luggage to the car?"

He nodded. "I've just finished cleaning up the kitchen."

She caught hold of his arm. "Are you sure you can't change her mind?"

"There's nothing I can do."

She frowned, her eyes glassy. "I'm going to miss that girl."

"I know. You could always visit her in Sydney."

"It's not the same and you know it."

"I'd better go help her pack the car."

"Jack." Her voice softened. "Have you asked her to stay?"

"It's complicated. Kate made the decision to leave today, even after knowing she was welcome to stay longer in our home."

"Okay, it's not my place to say anything or get involved, but I hope you know what you're doing."

He gave his aunt a brief hug. "I appreciate your concern but this decision is out of my hands and I'd better not keep her waiting any longer."

He left the kitchen, heading down the hall to Kate's room. A large suitcase was positioned near the door, the linen had been stripped from the bed, and the rest of the room was in immaculate order. She'd obviously spent a fair bit of time cleaning.

He carried the suitcase outside to her car, Doris's words lingering in his mind. He had the spare cash to clear all her debts but he understood her need to make the situation right herself. He didn't want her to feel beholden to him, either. *Lord, it's so hard to let her go and resist the temptation to step in and fix her financial situation. I don't know what the future holds, but I pray she will find a job quickly and make inroads into clearing all her debts.*

Kate opened a rear car door. "I'll store the suitcase here, since the back is already full."

"Sure." He hoisted the suitcase into the car and closed the door.

"Thanks for everything."

He nodded. "Would you like a cup of tea or coffee before you leave?"

"I'm good. I've already filled a thermos cup with leftover coffee from breakfast."

He shuffled from one foot to the other, weighing his words carefully. "Doris asked me if I could change your mind about leaving."

She lifted a brow. "What did you say?"

"I said the decision was out of my hands."

"I can't bear for Doris to learn the truth."

"You know she wouldn't judge you, or think less of you."

She dipped her head and shoved her hands in her coat pockets. "Yes, but it's bad enough that I've disappointed you. Doris doesn't need to know that I'm still suffering the consequences from my selfish behavior in Sydney."

"We all make mistakes."

"But some of us make more mistakes than others. I'd better get going."

"Have you checked you haven't left anything behind?"

"Yes, I triple-checked my room because I won't be able to come back anytime soon if I do leave something behind."

He paused, not sure if he'd like to hear the answer to his next question. "Do you want to come back and visit?"

She pressed her lips together, her gaze focused on her shoes. "You deserve someone much better than me."

He stepped forward. "But Kate—"

"No." She stepped back, raising her hands in the air. "You're not weakening my resolve to take care of my own problems. For too long I've relied on my father or Rodney to bail me out. This time I have to make things right myself."

He kicked a small stone into a nearby flower bed. "I get it, but it doesn't mean I like it."

"I'm really sorry, Jack. I don't know what else to say."

"Well, can I at least give you a hug before you leave?"

Her lip trembled and she nodded, moving into his open arms.

He held her close, her head resting against his chest. He stroked her hair, savoring the silky texture and inhaling her distinctive scent. It felt so right to hold her close in his arms, and he forced himself to pull away.

"I need to go."

He nodded. "I'm praying you'll have a safe trip."

"Thanks."

Doris walked over to Kate and gave her a warm hug. "I hope you'll visit again soon." She held Kate's hand, her eyes cloudy.

"I'll miss you." She squeezed Doris's hand before slipping into the driver's seat.

The engine roared to life. She reversed her car back onto the drive, waving in his direction before accelerating away toward the road.

Doris moved to his side and slipped her arm around his waist. "If it's meant to be, she'll return."

The car disappeared in a cloud of dust and he cleared his throat. He felt like she'd taken a piece of his heart with her.

He turned to Doris. "I have a lot of work to do in the orchards."

"Okay, I'll make something nice for lunch at midday."

"Thanks." He strode toward the shed, intent on focusing his attention on his work. She had left, and he had to learn to live without her.

Chapter 18

Kate placed a container of butter chicken in the microwave and set the timer. A week had passed since she'd left the farm. Her father was due home from work any minute and the rice was bubbling away in the cooker.

The garage door creaked open and she set the table in the dining room for two. Her mother had a dinner meeting with one of her social committees.

Her father strolled into the kitchen. "Something smells good."

"Butter chicken. From the store, of course."

He chuckled. "You underrate your abilities."

"Absolutely not. The gourmet deli makes it much better than I could." She poured a soda for her father. "I have good news. I was offered a job today."

"Really?" He smiled. "That was fast. Which one?"

"The three-month contract job that I really wanted. The

salary is excellent and there is potential for the job to become a permanent position."

"Congratulations. We can celebrate tonight. When do you start?"

"Monday. I will need to live with you and Mom for a while." Her first paycheck would arrive in time to pacify the debt collector.

He shrugged. "You're welcome here as long as you want. But is this what you want?"

She nodded. "My plan was to pick up a job when I returned to Sydney." The one thing she hadn't counted on was meeting a farmer who led her to question the wisdom of this decision way too often. If only she had kept track of her finances. A relationship with Jack was impossible now that her debt was out of control.

"What about Jack?"

She sucked in a deep breath. "He'll be fine now that his mother is home to take over the paperwork."

"I'm talking about your relationship with Jack. I can tell there was something going on between the two of you."

She ran her fingers through her hair, twisting a lock around her thumb. "It's complicated. We live different lives and I can't expect him to move to the city."

Her father looked thoughtful. "But I could see you living in the country. You've come home relaxed and more centered than I've seen you in a long time."

"That's probably because Rodney is no longer a part of my life. I think I always knew deep down that he wanted a trophy wife and didn't really love me."

"But Jack is different from Rodney. From what you've said, he is honest and has integrity."

"That's the problem. He doesn't deserve to be burdened with my problems."

"What do you mean? Has something happened?"

She leaned back on the counter. "I messed up big time and forgot about a store card I had maxed when I was with Rodney."

"Oh, Kate, you really need to learn to live within your means." He frowned. "Although I'm partly to blame because I spoiled you and bought you whatever you wanted when you were younger."

"We wouldn't be having this conversation if I'd married Rodney. And I fully intend to compensate you and Mom for the cost of the wedding. I know that will make Mom feel better."

"Your mother also played a role in the wedding fiasco. We've had a number of conversations and she knows I'm not happy about how hard she pushed you to get married."

She lifted the lid on the cooker and stirred the fluffy white rice. "I've forgiven Mom and I know she had good intentions. I really hurt her by running away from the church."

Her father placed a comforting hand on her shoulder. "I know you're hurting, too. Your mother is doing her best to get past it. She has finally realized that people have short memories and will soon forget her daughter left a multimillionaire at the altar. But don't push Jack away because you made a few mistakes. Have you contacted him?"

She sighed. "I sent him a message telling him I'd arrived home." And she'd thought about sending him a message today when she accepted the job offer.

"Why don't you call him?"

"And say what? That I'm starting a new job on Monday?" Fear curled in her belly. Could she gather the courage to speak to Jack and hear again his disappointment in her?

"You can tell him it's only a three month temp job." He paused. "Have you actually thought about why you were drawn to applying for temp work? I know the money is great but maybe your roots here aren't as deep as you want to believe?"

She had applied for the temp jobs before she received the letters from the debt collector. Had she subconsciously been hoping that she had a future with Jack? Was she really adverse to the idea of leaving Sydney and living on a farm permanently?

"Dad, I don't know." She spooned the rice and butter chicken onto their dinner plates. "I feel like everything is topsy-turvy and I can't think straight."

"Sweetheart, you can't hide behind your debt problems forever. This may sound harsh, but life moves on. Jack will probably wait only so long before he moves on, too."

Her father was right. Could Jack get past his disappointment? Did she deserve a second chance?

Jack finished polishing the bonnet of his white Jaguar. This afternoon he had a wedding booked at a local church followed by a Friday evening reception in Sunny Ridge.

His mother entered the shed. "I have lunch waiting for you."

"Thanks." His mother was helping him with the wedding and he'd made dinner reservations at a restaurant near the reception venue. She refused to go on the payroll for his car-hire business and he had to find creative ways to compensate her for her time and effort.

"I also have the food and drinks for this afternoon ready to go. Do you need me to iron one of your shirts?"

He shook his head. "I ironed last night, but thanks for the offer." Since his parents had returned home nearly two weeks ago, his mother had gone out of her way to spoil and look after him.

His mom stood beside him. "I worry about you."

He raised an eyebrow and continued polishing a side panel. "I'm fine, and the car-hire business is going great guns. I'm thinking about investing in another car."

"Really? Where exactly would you put it?"

He shrugged. "We could build another shed and use it to store apples when we start picking next year."

She laughed. "Jack, you'd have plenty of room in our existing sheds if you had fewer cars to garage. Anyway, I just opened the mail and we've got the green light to build a second house on the property. The town planners approved the initial plans drawn up by our architect."

He nodded. "That's good."

"Then why don't you sound more enthusiastic?"

"Why would I want to move out?" He shot his mom a cheeky grin. "You and Doris look after me too well."

Her eyes twinkled. "Maybe a girl called Kate could inspire you to move into your own place."

He dropped his gaze. "I don't think so."

"What happened?" Concern filled her voice. "I thought things were going well and she liked living here."

"It's a long story." A story he'd prefer not to talk about right now. He exerted more effort into his polishing and shuffled around to the back of the car.

"Have you been in touch since she left?"

He nodded. "She sent me a message when she arrived home, and then a second message to say she started a new job last week." He felt like a stone had lodged in his stomach. It hadn't taken her long to find a job and re-establish herself in her old life.

"Why don't you go to Sydney this weekend? It's the last weekend for a while where you don't have a Saturday wedding scheduled."

"What's the point? She has a job now and is getting on

with her life." A life without him. He clenched the cloth tighter in his fist.

"The point is, you can tell Kate how you feel and see how she responds. Maybe she misses you as much as you miss her."

His shoulders tensed and he quickened his circular movements with the cloth. "She's probably barely given me a second thought." She'd made it clear it was more important to repay her debt and return to her old life. She was used to a life of luxury, where money was plentiful and there to be spent.

How could he fit into Kate's world? He was a simple country bloke who liked living an uncomplicated life. He worked hard and had built up a tidy nest egg, but it was nothing compared to the wealth of Kate's family or ex-fiancé. How could he compete or be accepted into their affluent world?

His mother placed her hands on her hips and pinned him with a stern look. "I'm disappointed in you, Jack. I thought you had more guts than to give up so easily."

He stood, straightening his spine to his full height. "The truth is I don't think I have much of a chance. I don't think she's prepared to trade in her comfortable city life for a life with me." Was she prepared to curb her spending and live a modest life?

"Have you asked her to move here? Talked about commitment?"

"Mom, you're freaking me out with all this commitment talk. We haven't known each other that long—"

"But you've known each other long enough to really miss her now she has gone." She shook her head. "I'm sick of you moping around."

"I'm not moping. I've had a lot of work to do."

"You know, you can try and hide behind the work excuse but we both know the truth. Trust me. You'll live to regret it if you don't chase after her and see if you have a chance. What's the worst thing that could happen?"

He rubbed his hand through his hair. She could reject him like Amy did, because she's more infatuated with the bright lights of the city than with him. He didn't want to risk having his heart broken into pieces again, especially when he didn't think the odds were in his favor.

"Look, Jack, I have it on good authority from Doris that Kate has feelings for you. You need to see her again and see if you can work things out."

He started polishing the last couple of side panels. He had hoped Kate would want to stay in touch, although he wasn't a big fan of long-distance relationships. "Okay, I'll think about it."

"Good." A satisfied smile lit up his mother's face. "I'd hate to see you miss out on what could be the best thing to happen in your life." She placed her delicate hand on his shoulder. "Since you're nearly done here, I'll go back inside and put the kettle on for lunch. Promise me you will think about what I've said."

He nodded and she strode out of the shed.

Maybe his mother was right. He had unfinished business with Kate. What if she reciprocated his feelings and he didn't chase after her? Could he be missing out on a life of happiness with the woman he loved?

His pulse raced. He missed her like crazy because he loved her. He wanted to build the house for her, and hopefully in time have a few kids running around the orchards. They could deal with her debts together and work out a solution. Her determination to get a job and repay the loans proved she was serious about changing her life for the better.

He stood and wiped his hands on a clean cloth. He'd call

her later tonight to tell her he was going to Sydney tomorrow. He would do his best to woo the woman he loved and put his heart on the line. He'd hope and pray that the biggest gamble of his life would pay off big time.

Chapter 19

Kate parked her car in her parents' triple garage and stifled a yawn. She'd forgotten how exhausting it was to do the nine-to-five work routine combined with two hours of commuting time in heavy Sydney traffic. It was just after six on Friday night and all she wanted to do was curl up in bed and fall asleep.

She made her way into the house, kicking off her heels in the living room adjoining the kitchen. Her mother was busy in the kitchen, preparing their evening meal.

She greeted her mother and collapsed in a heap on a leather lounge.

"Are you okay? I bought a latte for you on my way home from the gym, in case you needed a pick me up."

"Thanks, Mom." She dragged herself to the kitchen, the enticing aroma of coffee waking her up.

"How's work going?"

"It's okay." After two weeks she was feeling sluggish

and hadn't done any exercise. She needed to go to the gym tomorrow morning and get her blood pumping through her body now that she'd returned to a sedentary desk job.

Last night she'd garnered the courage to visit Rodney's home and return the engagement ring. After a short conversation on his front doorstep, dominated by his tales from his European trip, she finally had the closure she'd been seeking. Now it was time to have the difficult discussion with her mother.

She retreated to the sofa and sipped her latte. "I visited Rodney last night."

"Really? That's great. What did he say?"

"He thanked me for returning the ring and made it clear he'd moved on with his life."

"Oh, I was hoping things could be different."

She curled her feet underneath her and met her mother's gaze. "You know I'm really sorry I embarrassed you at the church. One day I hope you can forgive me."

Her mother nodded. "It's been tough, but I'm trying really hard to get past it. At least my friends have finally stopped talking about it."

"I didn't mean to hurt and embarrass you."

"I know. Your father has been arguing your case for weeks and I'm kind of over it. I'm sorry I pressured you to marry Rodney. I should have listened to your concerns instead of brushing them off. Now can we put the whole sorry saga behind us?"

"Yes, and I know for sure that he was the wrong man for me."

"How?" Her eyes widened. "Did you have a fling with Megan's brother?"

"No, I wouldn't call it a fling but I did start dating Jack not long before I moved home."

"You really like him, don't you? That's why you've been looking miserable."

She concentrated on drinking her latte. "I messed everything up and I don't think he's interested in seeing me again."

"Have you contacted him?"

"I've sent him a couple of messages, but I don't think things will work out." She had to accept that she'd lost her opportunity with Jack. If only thoughts of him didn't plague her mind on a regular basis.

Jack turned his SUV off the busy highway and onto a leafy street in Sydney's North Shore. Stately homes lined each side of the road and he could almost smell the affluence of the quiet neighborhood. Before long he approached the circular drive of Kate's family home.

He couldn't help but remember the last time he had driven along this road in his Cadillac convertible. He shook his head. How life had changed in a few short months.

This morning he'd left the farm at dawn, unable to sleep in any later and anxious to see his beautiful Kate again. He'd thought about messaging her to say he'd be early but then decided to wait. Sydney traffic was unpredictable and, if no one was home, he could always call Kate and come back in a couple of hours.

He drew to a halt next to the front entry and stared up at the imposing two-story federation-style home. Immaculate gardens lined the drive and colorful roses bloomed in the early-afternoon sunlight.

He walked up the stone steps to the front entry and pressed the doorbell. A minute later Kate's father opened the door.

"Jack, good to see you." A broad smile covered his face.

"I'm a bit early and I hope I haven't disturbed you."

"Not at all." He took a step back. "Grab your bags from the car and come inside."

Jack ducked around to the back of his SUV. He swung his overnight bag over his shoulder and followed Kate's father into a long hallway. The end of the hall opened up into a large kitchen adjoining a sunny living room at the back of the house.

Her father strolled into the kitchen and opened the fridge. "Katie is at the gym doing a cycle class. She said she should be back in around half an hour."

"No worries. I don't mind waiting."

"Would you like a drink?"

"A soda would be good, thanks." Jack sat on a soft, cream-leather sofa that overlooked a spacious wooden deck and outdoor pool. A gazebo doubling as a barbecue area had been added to the end of the deck. An entertainer's paradise that his mother would love to live in, except a pool would attract unwanted snakes.

Kate's father poured two drinks and passed one to him before sitting in a chair opposite Jack. He crossed his ankle over his leg and relaxed back into his seat. "Well, I was wondering how long it would take you to visit Katie."

He raised an eyebrow. There was no point in delaying hearing the inevitable. If her father didn't approve of his intentions then he needed more time to convince him to change his mind. "And do you approve?"

He nodded. "You're a good man, Jack. I know you will look after my daughter and treat her well."

Jack sipped his drink. "I appreciate your support. Now I just have to convince Kate that she could be happy living in the country."

"She's been through a lot over the last few months."

He nodded.

"You have my blessing to whisk my daughter away to your farm."

"Thank you." He let out a deep breath. One less obstacle to overcome in his pursuit of Kate's heart.

Her father grinned. "I can see that she's happy with you. In a few months her temp job will be finished and she'll be free to move."

Temp job? Why hadn't Kate mentioned this aspect of her new job to him? And why had she let him believe she had a permanent job in Sydney? Doubts started to eat away at his confidence. "How long is her contract?"

"Three months. Didn't she tell you?" He shook his head. "She's playing her cards close to her chest but don't let that disrupt your plans."

He couldn't blame Kate for struggling to trust him. He squared his shoulders. He'd have to make sure she knew his intentions were genuine and he would never use her or hurt her like Rodney had done.

Kate's father continued in his booming voice. "But I'm confident you'll achieve the outcome you want and make my daughter a very happy girl."

Footsteps sounded on the polished floorboards in the hall and Kate appeared at the entrance to the room.

"Jack!"

He stood and she flew across the room, throwing her arms around his neck.

"You're early," she said.

His heart skipped a beat and he held her close, inhaling the earthy scent of her perspiration. "I wanted to surprise you."

She stepped back, her hand covering her mouth. "Oh, I'm sorry. I'm all hot and sweaty from the gym and I must look a wreck."

He laughed, his gaze taking in her lean body clothed in tight-fitting and damp workout gear. His smile widened. "You look great."

She pouted. "You're just saying that to be nice." She swiped a loose lock of hair back off her clammy forehead.

Her father stood. "I think I'll leave you kids to catch up." He shook Jack's hand. "It's good to see you again."

"Thanks for the chat," Jack said.

"No problem." Kate's father stashed his empty glass in the kitchen and left the room.

She spun around to face Jack. "What have you and my father been talking about?"

He grinned. "Nothing much and definitely nothing you need to worry about."

She wrinkled her brow. "Are you sure?"

"Perfectly sure," he said, holding her gaze. How he had missed staring into her eyes.

"Okay." She made her way into the kitchen and poured herself a tall glass of iced water. "I'm starved. Have you had lunch?"

He nodded and sat on a stool opposite her at the granite island in the center of the kitchen. "I ate on the way, but don't let me stop you from eating lunch."

"Okay." She rummaged through the fridge and pulled out various ingredients. "For some reason this class always makes me hungry."

"Maybe you push yourself too hard?"

She chuckled. "Hardly. I'm really out of condition when it comes to cycling."

"Have you missed the gym?" And missed all the other activities she was used to doing in the city?

She shrugged. "Yes and no. The gym has advantages and disadvantages."

She grabbed a loaf of bread and started making what looked like a salad sandwich with an unusual combination of ingredients. She opened a bottle of mayonnaise. "Did you have a good trip?"

"Sure did." He polished off the remainder of his drink. "I left early and made good time."

She sat on a stool beside him and devoured her sandwich. "I'll take a shower and clean up after I've eaten. Have you made any plans for the weekend?"

He nodded. "I hope you have something nice to wear in your wardrobe."

She lifted a brow. "Dinner tonight?"

"If that's okay with you?"

A bright smile lit up her beautiful face. Even with a face free of makeup, she looked like she'd stepped off the cover of a magazine.

"So Jack, where are we going?"

He held her gaze. "It's a surprise."

"Really? Will you give me a clue?"

"Okay." He paused, pondering her question. "We'll take a cab to the venue."

She playfully slapped his arm. "That's not a real clue because it doesn't tell me anything."

He shrugged. "You'll just have to wait and see."

"Please, one more clue."

"All right. I'm wearing a suit, if that helps you decide what to wear."

"Oh." Her eyes sparkled. "We're going somewhere fancy, and probably in the city since I know you hate driving in the city traffic."

He laughed. "Okay, enough clues. You'll just have to wait and see where the cab takes us."

She placed her empty plate in the sink. "I'll be back soon. Don't go anywhere."

He grinned. "Don't you worry, I'm not going anywhere." He had a good feeling that tonight would work out just fine.

Chapter 20

Kate smoothed the skirt of her red silk dress over her knees and stared out the cab window at the dazzling lights of the Sydney skyline.

Jack leaned closer and whispered in her ear. "Are you enjoying the view?"

She nodded and met his glittering gaze. "Are we dining in the city?"

He reached for her hand, entwining his fingers with hers. "We'll be there soon."

The cab crawled along in the heavy traffic, eventually moving on to the northern approaches of the harbor bridge. Brightly lit boats dotted the calm waters of the harbor and the Sydney Opera House glowed against the inky night sky.

She squeezed his hand. "Have I been to this place before?"

"I'm not sure." His smile widened. "But hopefully tonight will be a very memorable night."

She tilted her head to the side. "I'm dying of curiosity."

"Be patient." His eyes sparkled. "You won't have to wait much longer."

The cab cruised through the busy city streets and before long pulled to a halt near the Pitt Street Mall shopping precinct. Jack paid the driver and helped her out of the cab.

She looked up at the impressive height of the famous Sydney Tower and clapped her hands together. "Are we dining in the Tower restaurant?"

He nodded and gave her an indulgent smile before taking her hand and walking beside her to the entrance. "I'm glad you approve."

"The view is amazing. Have you been here before?"

"Once, for a friend's wedding reception. It was on Australia Day and we had a close-up view of the fireworks display."

"Wow. You know, I haven't been here for a few years." She managed to keep pace with Jack in her two-inch heels and they stopped at an elevator leading up to the tower. "This is a wonderful surprise."

His eyes twinkled. "You're welcome. And you look absolutely breathtaking."

"Thanks." Her heart skipped a beat as she took in his dark suit and elegant blue tie. "And you look great. I like your suit."

He stood taller and squeezed her hand. "I'm glad you approve."

They rode two different elevators and finally entered the classy restaurant. Panoramic windows provided an incredible outlook of the harbor and outer-city suburbs. The sky was clear and a few distinctive stars sparkled near a glowing half moon.

A waiter led them to a window table. Kate gasped, her eyes glued to the fabulous view through the glass beside her while the waiter placed a white, starched-linen napkin on her lap.

"Jack, this is so beautiful." She turned to face him. "I don't know what to say."

His intense gaze seemed to drink her in. "I think the view opposite me looks pretty good, too."

She laughed. "Flattery will get you everywhere. You're saying all the right things to charm me tonight."

His eyes widened. "Well, I'm glad you're happy." He passed her a menu. "What takes your fancy?"

She perused the leather-bound menu. No prices were listed and she didn't want to think about how much this dinner was costing Jack. "Oysters to start would be nice. Definitely Oysters Kilpatrick and I think I'll also have the New York steak, medium."

He smiled. "I'll have the same." He signaled a waiter and placed their order.

She sat back in the comfortable chair, her gaze drawn to the twinkling lights of the city skyline below. "This is an incredible night."

"I hope so." His warm gaze met hers. "I've missed you."

"Me, too." She'd missed the easy conversation they'd always shared, and how she could talk with him for hours about nearly anything.

"How's work?"

She shrugged. "It's okay. Work is work, I guess."

"Your father mentioned you signed a three-month contract."

She lowered her lashes. "I'm keeping my options open."

"Am I one of your options?" His light tone couldn't disguise the emotion in his voice.

Her gaze flew to his face and an earnest look entered his eyes.

"Do you want to be?" Her quiet question hung in the air.

He leaned over and reached for her left hand, his fingertips gently caressing her fingers. "I was going to wait until after we'd eaten, but since you've brought up the subject."

She opened her mouth but no words formed on her lips. What was he suggesting? Her heart swelled and hope filled every fiber in her body.

His steady gaze locked with hers. "Kate, I love you and I hope you feel the same way."

She nodded, nibbling on her lower lip.

"And how exactly do you feel?"

She widened her eyes, encouraged by his warm gaze. "I love you, Jack. I have for a while, but after what I've done I've been hesitant to put my feelings into words."

He nodded. "I know I wasn't as understanding as I could have been when you told me about the debt."

She sucked in a deep breath. "And I'm sorry I didn't tell you about the temp job earlier. I have this enormous debt to manage and we live totally different lives...."

"It doesn't have to be that way." He reached into a pocket in the lining of his jacket and pulled out a small, black-velvet jewelry case.

She gasped. "Oh, Jack."

He opened the lid of the case and a diamond solitaire gold ring sparkled against a black-velvet backdrop.

Her pulse raced. "The ring is exquisite."

"It belonged to my great-grandmother. It probably needs resizing but I was too impatient to wait." He leaped out of his seat and dropped on one knee beside her. "My beautiful Kate, will you do me the honor of becoming my wife?"

Tears of happiness threatened to fall as she experienced the intensity of Jack's love for her. She nodded. "Yes."

He cradled her face between his hands and placed a sweet kiss on her lips. She parted her mouth and welcomed the intimacy as he deepened the kiss.

Moments later he drew back and a round of applause erupted from nearby tables. Congratulations were offered before the other diners returned to their meals and gave them some privacy. A waiter served their oysters before discreetly departing.

She blinked away the moisture in her eyes. "Wow, Jack. We're now engaged!"

He stood and slipped back into his chair. "Let's see how this ring fits."

She offered her left hand and he slid the diamond engagement ring on her finger, the band feeling a little loose as he moved the ring over her knuckle.

She giggled. "Nearly a perfect fit. One size smaller is all we need."

He laughed. "At least you can wear it. I was worried it would be too small."

She gave him a mock frown. "You don't think I have small and delicate fingers?"

He lifted her hand and kissed each finger tip, one at a time. "You have perfect hands."

She giggled. "You're too kind. I've said yes so you can tell me the truth now."

"I am telling the truth and I think we should eat our oysters." He scooped an oyster out of a shell and held out his spoon. "For you."

"Okay." She narrowed her eyes. "Be careful, I don't want to wear the oyster."

He laughed. "You could move a bit closer."

She leaned toward him and he slid the oyster between her lips. The tangy sauce exploded in her mouth and she closed her eyes, savoring the delicious flavors.

"Was that good?"

She nodded. "But I can feed myself, you know."

He raised an eyebrow. "Where's your sense of adventure?"

"Actually, I was thinking we should talk more about our future. When exactly were you thinking we could get married? I don't want to burden you with my debts and we will need to set a date at some stage."

He grinned. "I don't care about your debt and I'd love to get married as soon as possible. Why wait?"

She smiled, admiring the glittering diamond on her finger. "I would feel better if I finished this work contract first."

"At least it's only for three months and we do need time to organize the wedding."

"I'd like to get married in Snowgum Creek."

His eyes widened. "Really? You don't want a big Sydney wedding?"

She shook her head. "The last time I tried that it didn't work out well for me."

He grinned. "I can't say I'm too upset about that."

"A simple country wedding would be nice. I don't want a big fuss." She sampled another oyster. "Anyway, it was my mother's idea last time to turn it into a big production."

"I'm not keen on a big production."

She straightened her shoulders. "This time we're going to do it our way. We will make the decisions together."

"Agreed." He reached for her hand and inspected her new ring. "Interference from well-meaning family will not be tolerated."

"And we'll also need to work out where we're going to live."

He looked up and held her gaze. "Are you happy to move to Snowgum Creek?"

She nodded. "But we need to think about having our

own place. As much as I like your family, I don't want to impose on them."

"And you don't think I've already given this some thought?"

She sipped her sparkling water. "Well, I wasn't expecting a wedding proposal tonight." She had hoped he'd propose at some stage, but had never expected that tonight would be the night.

He ate his last oyster and set his plate aside. "I was going to keep this as a surprise, but since you don't seem to like surprises…"

"Jack, please tell me." She looked him straight in the eye. "What are you planning?"

"We're going to build a house on the farm. For us and for any little ones who may come along."

Her heart swelled. "Oh, Jack, this sounds perfect." Happy tears pricked the corners of her eyes. "I'm so blessed to have a man like you."

He shook his head. "No, I'm the blessed one."

Chapter 21

Kate adjusted her bridal veil over the beaded bodice of her cream silk wedding dress. She stood in the entrance to Snowgum Creek Community Church and glanced at her father.

His eyes twinkled. "Are you ready?"

She grinned as their photographer snapped another photo. "Yes, and this time I'm not going anywhere."

His smile widened. "That's my girl, and you've chosen well. Jack is a good man and I trust he will take good care of you."

"I know he will." She tucked her hand through the crook of his elbow. "Let's do it."

She took small steps as she walked toward the short aisle, her sleek, fitted skirt swirling around her legs.

She caught Jack's eye as he stood at the front of the church, wearing a stylish suit.

Her pulse raced and she beamed him a big smile.

He winked and a broad grin spread over his handsome face.

The gentle organ music floated around her as she held Jack's gaze and gradually moved closer to his side.

She reached the front of the church and he grasped her hand, whispering in her ear. "You look gorgeous."

Her heart skipped a beat and she squeezed his hand. "So do you."

Her father gave her a brief kiss on the cheek before standing aside.

She met Jack's loving gaze, the quiet words spoken by their pastor soothing her nerves. Today was like a fairy tale come true and she marveled in the knowledge she was marrying an amazing man who loved her.

She repeated her vows and tried to absorb every moment of the beautiful ceremony. Her mother sat in the front row beside her father, a big smile on her face.

The pastor eventually pronounced them man and wife.

Jack gently lifted her veil. "I've been waiting all day for this moment."

A slow shiver raced through her body. "So have I."

His mouth descended and his lips met hers in an incredible toe-tingling kiss.

She wrapped her arms around his muscular torso and savored every moment of their brief kiss. Applause erupted from the wedding guests, bringing her back down to earth.

The remainder of the ceremony passed in a blur of activity. She took a seat at a small table and signed her wedding certificate with Megan as her witness. The photographer issued directions and she posed for more pictures, content to be snuggled up next to Jack.

Before long the ceremony drew to a close and she was walking back down the aisle on Jack's arm, pausing for the photographer to take photos before exiting the church.

She stepped outside the church with Jack and the late-afternoon sun filtered through the trees. Well-wishers covered her and Jack in rose petals.

She smiled at Jack, plucking a rose petal out of his neatly groomed hair. "We did it."

He wrapped his arm around her shoulders, pulling her closer to his side. "I'm a very happy man, Mrs. Bradley."

She thanked God for bringing this incredible man into her life and continued to smile for the cameras. All her dreams had come true today.

* * * * *

REQUEST YOUR FREE BOOKS!

2 FREE INSPIRATIONAL NOVELS
PLUS 2
FREE
MYSTERY GIFTS

Love Inspired

YES! Please send me 2 FREE Love Inspired® novels and my 2 FREE mystery gifts (gifts are worth about $10). After receiving them, if I don't wish to receive any more books, I can return the shipping statement marked "cancel." If I don't cancel, I will receive 6 brand-new novels every month and be billed just $4.74 per book in the U.S. or $5.24 per book in Canada. That's a savings of at least 21% off the cover price. It's quite a bargain! Shipping and handling is just 50¢ per book in the U.S. and 75¢ per book in Canada.* I understand that accepting the 2 free books and gifts places me under no obligation to buy anything. I can always return a shipment and cancel at any time. Even if I never buy another book, the two free books and gifts are mine to keep forever.

105/305 IDN F49N

Name _____ (PLEASE PRINT) _____

Address _____ Apt. # _____

City _____ State/Prov. _____ Zip/Postal Code _____

Signature (if under 18, a parent or guardian must sign)

Mail to the Harlequin® Reader Service:
IN U.S.A.: P.O. Box 1867, Buffalo, NY 14240-1867
IN CANADA: P.O. Box 609, Fort Erie, Ontario L2A 5X3

Are you a subscriber to Love Inspired books
and want to receive the larger-print edition?
Call 1-800-873-8635 or visit www.ReaderService.com.

* Terms and prices subject to change without notice. Prices do not include applicable taxes. Sales tax applicable in N.Y. Canadian residents will be charged applicable taxes. Offer not valid in Quebec. This offer is limited to one order per household. Not valid for current subscribers to Love Inspired books. All orders subject to credit approval. Credit or debit balances in a customer's account(s) may be offset by any other outstanding balance owed by or to the customer. Please allow 4 to 6 weeks for delivery. Offer available while quantities last.

Your Privacy—The Harlequin® Reader Service is committed to protecting your privacy. Our Privacy Policy is available online at www.ReaderService.com or upon request from the Harlequin Reader Service.
We make a portion of our mailing list available to reputable third parties that offer products we believe may interest you. If you prefer that we not exchange your name with third parties, or if you wish to clarify or modify your communication preferences, please visit us at www.ReaderService.com/consumerchoice or write to us at Harlequin Reader Service Preference Service, P.O. Box 9062, Buffalo, NY 14269. Include your complete name and address.

LIDIR13R

REQUEST YOUR FREE BOOKS!

2 FREE INSPIRATIONAL NOVELS
PLUS 2
FREE
MYSTERY GIFTS

Love Inspired.
HISTORICAL
INSPIRATIONAL HISTORICAL ROMANCE

YES! Please send me 2 FREE Love Inspired® Historical novels and my 2 FREE mystery gifts (gifts are worth about $10). After receiving them, if I don't wish to receive any more books, I can return the shipping statement marked "cancel." If I don't cancel, I will receive 4 brand-new novels every month and be billed just $4.74 per book in the U.S. or $5.24 per book in Canada. That's a savings of at least 21% off the cover price. It's quite a bargain! Shipping and handling is just 50¢ per book in the U.S. and 75¢ per book in Canada.* I understand that accepting the 2 free books and gifts places me under no obligation to buy anything. I can always return a shipment and cancel at any time. Even if I never buy another book, the two free books and gifts are mine to keep forever.

102/302 IDN F5CY

Name _____ (PLEASE PRINT) _____

Address _____ Apt. # _____

City _____ State/Prov. _____ Zip/Postal Code _____

Signature (if under 18, a parent or guardian must sign) _____

Mail to the Harlequin® Reader Service:
IN U.S.A.: P.O. Box 1867, Buffalo, NY 14240-1867
IN CANADA: P.O. Box 609, Fort Erie, Ontario L2A 5X3

**Want to try two free books from another series?
Call 1-800-873-8635 or visit www.ReaderService.com.**

---

* Terms and prices subject to change without notice. Prices do not include applicable taxes. Sales tax applicable in N.Y. Canadian residents will be charged applicable taxes. Offer not valid in Quebec. This offer is limited to one order per household. Not valid for current subscribers to Love Inspired Historical books. All orders subject to credit approval. Credit or debit balances in a customer's account(s) may be offset by any other outstanding balance owed by or to the customer. Please allow 4 to 6 weeks for delivery. Offer available while quantities last.

Your Privacy—The Harlequin® Reader Service is committed to protecting your privacy. Our Privacy Policy is available online at www.ReaderService.com or upon request from the Harlequin Reader Service.

We make a portion of our mailing list available to reputable third parties that offer products we believe may interest you. If you prefer that we not exchange your name with third parties, or if you wish to clarify or modify your communication preferences, please visit us at www.ReaderService.com/consumerschoice or write to us at Harlequin Reader Service Preference Service, P.O. Box 9062, Buffalo, NY 14269. Include your complete name and address.

LIHDIR13R

Reader Service.com

Manage your account online!
- Review your order history
- Manage your payments
- Update your address

> ### We've designed
> ### the Harlequin® Reader Service
> ### website just for you.

Enjoy all the features!
- Reader excerpts from any series
- Respond to mailings and
  special monthly offers
- Discover new series available to you
- Browse the Bonus Bucks catalog
- Share your feedback

Visit us at:
ReaderService.com